Charles Knowles Bolton

Brookline

the history of a favored town

Charles Knowles Bolton

Brookline
the history of a favored town

ISBN/EAN: 9783337313562

Printed in Europe, USA, Canada, Australia, Japan

Cover: Foto ©Andreas Hilbeck / pixelio.de

More available books at **www.hansebooks.com**

BROOKLINE

THE HISTORY OF A FAVORED TOWN

BY

CHARLES KNOWLES BOLTON

Librarian of the Public Library

ILLUSTRATED

BROOKLINE, MASSACHUSETTS

PUBLISHED BY C. A. W. SPENCER

1897

May 17. 1714 Att a Town Meeting Legally Warned.

Voted, In that upon deliberation the Inhabitants declined sending a Representative upon the Acc't of their building a Meeting House and the great charges thereof for such a Poor Little Town, We, the Inhabitants, do desire and pray this Hon'd. House would excuse us this year. . . . . Town Records, Page 101.

Books by Mr. Bolton.

For sale by C. A. W. Spencer, Brookline, Mass., and by their publishers.

On the Wooing of Martha Pitkin, being a versified narrative of the time of the regicides in colonial New England. THIRD EDITION. Small 8º, eighteenth century binding, 75 c. Published by Copeland and Day, 69 Cornhill, Boston.

An historical romance of early days in Connecticut.

The Love-Story of Ursula Wolcott, a tale in verse of the time of the " great revival " in New England. FIRST THOUSAND. Small 4º, hand made paper, deckled edges, with illustrations and cover design by Miss Ethel Reed. $1.00. Published by Lamson, Wolffe & Co., 6 Beacon Street, Boston.

Ursula Wolcott was the granddaughter of Martha Pitkin.

Saskia the wife of Rembrandt. Fifteen illustrations from Rembrandt's portraits, and from scenes in Amsterdam. 8º, bound in cloth. $1.50. Published by T. Y. Crowell & Co., 100 Purchase Street, Boston.

A picture of the home life of Rembrandt in the quaint Dutch city of Amsterdam during the years when it led the world in discovery, commerce, and art.

The librarian's duty as a citizen. Pamphlet. By mail, 10 c.

What the small town may do for itself. Pamphlet. By mail, 25 c.

Brookline : The history of a favored town. 750 copies printed. Illustrated. $2.00. Published by C. A. W. Spencer, Harvard Square, Brookline.

PREFACE.

As an important residence district in one of the oldest, wealthiest, and largest centers of population of the United States, Brookline must always have a certain claim to distinction, much like that of Belgravia in London. As a small town, nearly surrounded by a great municipality, yet maintaining through the loyalty of its citizens a corporate existence, Brookline has a further claim to consideration. Never were the affairs of a town, spending nearly a million dollars a year, more quietly nor more ably administered.

There has been heretofore no chronological, illustrated history of Brookline in the hands of the people. The present little book has grown from materials collected during the preparation of a paper, which was read before the Hannah Goddard chapter of the Daughters of the American Revolution, the First Parish club, the All Saints Parish club, and the Isaac Gardner chapter of the Daughters of the Revolution, during the winter of 1896–97.   It has been thought best not to refer constantly to authorities; but to the works of Rev. John Pierce, Alfred D. Chandler, Esq., Bradford Kingman, Esq., Mr. B. F. Baker, and particularly Miss Harriet F. Woods every student of town history must turn.   To these, to the writers of the invaluable essays printed by the Brookline Historical Publication Society, and to Dr. Augustine Shurtleff, Mr. Daniel S. Sanford, Mr. C. A. W. Spencer, Miss Emma G. Cummings, Mr. Reginald Heber Howe, Jr., Mr. Hector Hughes, Miss Ellen Chase, Mr. George F. Joyce, and to many others, I make cordial acknowledgment.

A dedication has hardly become customary in town histories, and yet I cannot forego the opportunity to associate with these pages the name of Rev. Howard N. Brown, now minister of King's chapel, Boston, but for many years minister of the First Parish, Brookline, and a trustee of the Public Library.

C. K. B.

CONTENTS.

ILLUSTRATIONS.

THE HOME OF PETER ASPINWALL, ASPINWALL AVENUE.

Built in 1660.   Taken down in 1891.

BROOKLINE:

THE HISTORY OF A FAVORED TOWN.

"THE HAMLET OF MUDDY RIVER."

November 13, 1705, the date which marks the incorporation of Brookline as a town, stands midway between that time when the Puritans, seekers for religious freedom, first settled the land, and the days which opened the struggle for political independence. From the western shore of the peninsula called "Boston," that is, from the Common, water stretched for two miles to the westward. Beyond this expanse of water which was hemmed in on the south by the Roxbury shore there arose four wooded hills — at the right, what are now Corey Hill and Babcock Hill, at the left, Aspinwall Hill and Fisher Hill. Between these there were valleys sloping down to the marshes which bordered Muddy River. This beautiful wooded country was to the Boston emigrant what Oklahoma has recently been to the western pioneer. It was a land to be had for the asking.

In 1635 the Boston authorities granted to Rev. John Cotton, "our teacher," an allotment sufficient for a farm. It lay about the present Cypress street ; or more definitely, it contained land west of the parkway bounded southerly by the Boston & Albany circuit, and northerly by Brook street and Harvard avenue. The western boundary was at least as distant as Gardner road.

Another of the early proprietors was Robert Hull, whose son John, the famous mint-master of Boston, inherited his estate. From John the property passed to his more famous son-in-law, Chief Justice Sewall. This land centered about Beacon street east of Harvard street.

In looking over the old records, it seems as if every resident of Boston, who was not possessed of abnormal modesty, asked for an allotment in what was then called "the hamlet of Muddy River." Nearly one hundred persons quickly received their portion of land, varying in extent according to the numbers which constituted their families. The grants were made more rapidly than the surveyors could lay them out. Notices like this on the records are not infrequent :—

"Our brother Peter Oliver hath granted unto him sixty acres of land at Muddy River, if it be there to be had, of the which there is granted some marsh, if there be any there, always provided that those grants before granted are first served."

But as was natural, many had to wait for their property to be surveyed. Thomas Scottow was granted land for three heads in February, 163⅞, and in December, 1639, we find him petitioning for land for five heads, his family having increased meantime to that number. Other records show that the town officials of Boston often granted more than they meant to, but found it inconvenient to reduce the amount.

Among the early names in these records, probably the only ones still to be found represented in this neighborhood are Davis, Griggs, Winchester, and White.

A cart bridge was ordered March 4, 1634/5, to be paid for by Boston, Roxbury, Dorchester, Watertown and Cambridge. Brookline was thus a pivotal point. All the traffic going toward the west passed out through Newbury street and Orange street (together a part of the present Washington street, Boston), over Boston Neck (Washington street near Dover street), through Roxbury street, which was then called " the Cambridge road," past the First Church where the apostle Eliot preached, to the present Roxbury Crossing, thence along the highway now called Tremont street and Huntington avenue, up through what is now the village, and out

Walnut street and Heath street (then together forming the old Sherburne road).

The old Sherburne road lay along the southern slope of Fisher Hill. The depression between the northeastern slope and Aspinwall Hill formed the bed of the Village Brook, beside which now run the tracks of the Boston & Albany circuit. Between Aspinwall Hill and Corey Hill the early settlers laid out the road to Brighton and Watertown, the present Washington street; and between Corey Hill and Babcock Hill they made a road to Cambridge. An early statement in the records that the road to Cambridge, which perhaps represented the modern Harvard street, was to be blazoned through the trees, gives in one word a vivid picture of the woodland that covered the town. These roads had a common starting point which became "the village." Here was built the Punch Bowl Tavern, from which Brookline came to be known as the "Punch Bowl Village." The tavern stood on the eastern corner of Pearl and Washington streets. To the original building additions were made from time to time, as traffic through the town increased. During the revolutionary period and earlier a well managed tavern gave the town in which it stood a more than local reputation, and the traveler's diary usually recorded the name of the inn at which he tarried. The Punch Bowl was famous in western and northern New England until the nineteenth century. Beneath its overhanging second story a seat invited loiterers. Elm trees and a pump were before the door. But most conspicuous was the tavern sign, upon which were depicted a punch bowl and ladle, shaded by the cooling leaves of a fruitful lemon tree. What proportion of the refreshing draughts came from the juice of the lemon only the departed travelers could tell. The old building was taken down about 1830.

In these early days an Indian fort stood on what is now the eastern corner of Beacon and

Powell streets; it covered one-eighth of an acre, was surrounded by a ditch about three feet deep, and by a parapet nearly three feet high.

Mrs. Lee, in her "Naomi," writes thus of Brookline in 1660: "The town of Roxbury possessed beautiful farms, but beyond that, Brookline, then called Muddy River, deserved not the appellation of the pleasure-garden of Norfolk, although its wild beauties far surpassed those which the hand of man has given it as a dowry. It was principally used for grazing cattle, for which its meadows and sheltered nooks of rich pasturage were particularly adapted. At this time there were a few houses at what was afterwards known as the Punch-Bowl Village, and a road from thence to Cambridge."

Many of the citizens of Boston to whom were made grants of land, did not come to Brookline to live. John Josselyn writes in 1675: "Two miles from the town, in a place called Muddy River, the inhabitants have farms, to which belong rich, arable grounds and meadows, where they keep their cattle in summer, and bring them to Boston in the winter." From this custom, perhaps, came the name "Boston Commons," occasionally applied to Muddy River.

In 1686 the inhabitants of Muddy River petitioned to be allowed to manage their own affairs, and to be exempt from rates to the town of Boston. This was granted, with the provision that they erect a school-house within one year, and provide an able reading and writing master.

The people were either unable to pay the rates, the wealthier Boston land owners never having had a residence in the town, or they were beginning to show that independence which has characterized the town ever since, for we soon find them petitioning for greater liberties. These attempts annoyed the Boston authorities, who voted in 1700 that the people of Muddy River should pay their rates for the future. In 1705, however, circumstances seem to have favored another appeal. Whether this was due or not to the fact that the town clerk, Samuel Sewall, was not only the son of Chief Justice Sewall, a member of the council at that time, but also the son-in-law of the governor, Joseph Dudley, it cannot with certainty be said; but the adoption of the name "Brookline" for the territory formerly known as Muddy River, at least implies a compliment to the chief justice.

On Monday, June 20, 1687, Judge Sewall writes in his famous diary: "Went to Muddy River with Mr. Gore and Eliot to take a Plot of Brooklin." And on Wednesday, June 22, "Went to Muddy River. Mr. Gore finishes compassing the land with his plain table; I do it chiefly that I may know my own, it lies in so many nooks and corners."

Judge Sewall's farm, called "Brookline," was on the eastern side of what is now Naples road, and had for its boundary Smelt Brook. Part of this farm was inherited by a descendant, the wife of E. K. Wolcott, and the Hales map of 1820 has the words "Woolcott Farm" close by the line of the brook. Smelt Brook starts at the foot of Corey Hill, near the present Winchester street, crosses Harvard street, follows in a general way the direction of Naples road, crosses Commonwealth avenue and enters the Charles. As Chief Justice Sewall was a man of influence at the time, and as his farm was called "Brookline," it very likely seemed to the inhabitants of Muddy River, that the suggestion of "Brookline" for a name for the town was a compliment both to the chief justice and to the governor, which would further their desire for civic independence.

In the year 1700 there were about fifty families in the town; the number did not increase materially until near the beginning of the next century when the country-house population began to be a feature of Brookline. The original meeting-house, which first stood on the present parsonage grounds of the Unitarian church on Walnut street (opposite Perrin place, now called Maple terrace), was not only the geographical center, but the social center of the town. Nearby the town hall and the school-house were built.

The poverty of the town at this time was as conspicuous as its wealth has come to be in these days. It is said that today the yearly revenues and expenditures of Brookline are about double the revenues and expenditures of the State of New Hampshire. In contrast with this, the first

struggle to build a meeting-house may be of
interest. In 1705, when the town was incorporated, the people were enjoined to build a
meeting-house and to obtain an orthodox minister in three years. In 1709 Brookline sent a
petition to the governor, Joseph Dudley, saying
that they wished three years more to settle a
minister. On account of the extraordinary
province taxes and their contribution toward the
support of the ministry in the south end of
Roxbury where the people worshipped — "our
most remote ffamily resorting to the new meeting-
house" — a petition in November, 1710, for
further time was favorably considered. On
June 10, 1713, another grant of time was made.
Finally, the meeting-house was raised, November
10, 1714. It contained in all fourteen seats built
around the wall; a flight of stairs on either side
led to the gallery for men and the gallery for
women. Thirty-nine members constituted the
first organization.

HOUSE OF EDWARD DEVOTION, WASHINGTON STREET.

He died here in 1774.

The Rev. James Allen was ordained the first minister of this, the town's church, November 5, 1718, and preached until his death in February, 1747. His successors to 1850 have been : —

2. Rev. Cotton Brown, ordained October 26, 1748; died April 13, 1751.

3. Rev. Nathaniel Potter, ordained November 19, 1755 ; dismissed June 17, 1759.

4. Rev. Joseph Jackson, ordained April 9, 1760 ; died July 22, 1796.

5. Rev. John Pierce, ordained March 15, 1797; died August 24, 1849.

On Monday, December 6, 1847, the town voted to give to the First Parish a quit-claim deed, releasing in fee simple all the town's right in and to the land on which the meeting-house now stands. The affairs of the First Parish since this date belong more properly to church history. In this deed are the words: "The town is to covenant that the triangular lot of land lying east of the estate of John E. Thayer shall forever remain open and unencumbered." So that this, the first village green, and the site of the first town school, and later of the "brick school," still remains open.

Returning for a moment to the days of the Rev. James Allen, it was voted in 1717, the year before his ordination, that the "ministers sallary of £80 pounds be raised by an equall and Proportionable Rate Levyed on the Inhabitants." And all money contributed by strangers was to go into the town treasury. These were the days when charity began at home.

In his sermons Mr. Allen was a careful, methodical divine ; he pressed home the truths for which such events as the earthquake of October 29, 1727, and the death of Mr. Samuel Aspinwall in 1732, prepared his listeners.

In July, 1743, Mr. Allen wrote a semi-public letter expressing his joy that there were " scores of persons under awakenings " in his parish, as a result of the Whitefield revivals. Some time afterward he grew out of sympathy with the "delusion," as he called it, and said that they were "upon the devil's ground." He spoke harshly of them, and "lived at variance with one of his neighbors almost four years, and declined to make it up with him." Ebenezer Kendrick, Nathaniel Shepard, John Seaver, Jr., Elhanan Winchester, Jr., Richard Seaver, and Dudley Boylston, Jr., withdrew from the church and joined the "New Lights." They held worship in the Shepard house, later known as the Dana house, which stood near the western Public Library gate. Mr. Allen tried to do his duty during these times of unrest, although the worry undermined his health.

The above Elhanan Winchester's son, of the same name, was born in 1751. He began his remarkable career as a preacher in the New Light faith, but changed to the Baptist communion, and finally to Universalism. His reputation grew year by year, as he went from city to city in this country and in Europe. He wrote many hymns, and was a friend of the leading clergymen of the last half of the 18th century, and also of such men as John Jay, Timothy Pickering and Dr. Benjamin Rush. He died April 18, 1797, loved by many Brookline friends who could not follow his teachings.

The Rev. Joseph Jackson, minister of the First Parish during this period, a diffident, reserved man, suffered from the movement in which Mr. Winchester was a leader. Dr. Pierce, his successor, was the first minister of the church to represent the Unitarian spirit, although he never allowed himself to discuss creeds or differences in faith.

DEVOTION HOUSE, HARVARD STREET.

Built by John Devotion in the year 1680. The estate in modern times known as the Babcock Farm.

To face p. 25.

In the early days, among prominent families were the Boylstons, the Goddards, the Aspinwalls, the Devotions, the Winchesters, the Gardners, the Sharps, the Davises, and the Whites. Dr. Thomas Boylston and his son, Dr. Zabdiel, of inoculation fame, are associated with the early history of the Henry Lee place on Boylston street, north of the reservoir. Peter Boylston was a grandfather of President John Adams. Memorial Hall at Harvard contains a number of fine portraits of members of the family.

The Goddards came from a well-known family in London; William Goddard settled in Watertown, and was a teacher of Latin there. His great-grandson John, who lived near the present Goddard avenue, did conspicuous service during the Revolution. A branch of the family in England is now prominent in the church.

The Aspinwalls, who came from near Liverpool, and settled about the present Aspinwall
avenue, across the brook from the Cotton estate,
are like the Goddards, still represented here, and
like the Boylstons, have furnished distinguished
physicians to the town.

The Sharps, who lived on the western side of
the present Harvard street, near Auburn, did
service in the early Indian wars. Lieutenant
John Sharp, of Captain Wadsworth's company,
marching in 1676 from Marlboro to Sudbury to
attack King Philip, was drawn into an ambush ;
after four hours of fighting the company was
driven back in confusion by fire started among
the dry leaves by the Indians, and both Wadsworth and Sharp were killed.

The Brookline branch of the Gardners came
from Cambridge at an early date. They were
represented in the Revolution by Isaac Gardner,
whose death on the 19th of April, fighting
against the king's troops, caused so much com-

ment in England, and by Colonel Thomas Gardner, of the Cambridge branch, who died from wounds received at Bunker Hill. Isaac Gardner lived on Brighton street, now Chestnut Hill avenue.

The Davises of the present day trace descent from Ebenezer Davis of Roxbury, whose son, Deacon Ebenezer, in the latter part of the 17th century, purchased from the Cotton family land on both sides of the present Washington street in the village. Their house stood on the eastern side of Kent street. Robert S. Davis, the Boston bookseller, published Miss Woods' Historical Sketches of Brookline in 1874. Other members of the family were General P. Stearns Davis and Hon. Thomas A. Davis, Mayor of Boston.

The land about Naples road, now called the Babcock farm, was once owned by John Devotion, a prominent man in the town. His son Edward, who is said to have lived on the farm in summer and in the village in winter, left property to the schools. In 1762 it amounted to £739-4s. The Edward Devotion School, which stands on the farm, is a worthy memorial of his public spirit. Descendants of other names are still living.

The Griggs family comes from Joseph Griggs of Roxbury, who married, in 1653, Mary, daughter of Griffin Craft, whose family also became associated with the town. A son, Ichabod, a man of wealth and influence, was the father of Samuel Griggs, who acquired Captain John Winchester's place on Harvard street, beyond Beacon street.

William Hyslop, a poor Scotch peddler, came to America some years before the Revolution, and having amassed a fortune purchased the Boylston place on Fisher Hill. His daughter married Governor Increase Sumner. A son, David, who inherited the place, was very peculiar. He disliked music and called anthems "tantrums ; " come was pronounced "tum," and study

HOUSE OF EROZOMON DREW, NEAR NEWTON STREET.

Built about 1693. Afterwards owned by Deacon Ebenezer Craft. Torn down in 1873.

From " The Crafts Family." Lent by W. F. Crafts, Esq.

To face p. 29.

was always "tuddy." In 1821 he gave a grand dinner party for President John Adams, who, although aged and feeble, had expressed a desire to see once more the house in which his mother was born.

Robert Harris, an early settler near the Roxbury line, in "Putterham," the southwestern corner of the town, was the great great grandfather of Rev. William Harris, D.D., president of Columbia College, N. Y., 1811–1829.

James and Elinor Clark lived in a house near the eastern corner of the present Harvard street and Harvard avenue, and owned the surrounding land. Their grandson, Deacon Samuel, built the first meeting-house on the old Sherburne road, and also the Clark house at the corner of Walnut and Chestnut streets. He owned the garrison house in the rear. Miss Sarah and Miss Susan Clark of the present generation gave many interesting old manuscripts to the Public Library.

Captain Timothy Corey of Weston married Elizabeth Griggs of Brookline and came here to live just before the Revolution, in which he took part. His sons, Elijah and Timothy, were interested in the revivals of the time, and became deacons in the Baptist church. The family is still represented here.

The Winchesters, famous in Brookline religious annals and even in the greater world without, were of Welsh origin, like the Davises. John Winchester, first representative from Brookline to the general court, lived on land stretching from the Cambridge road, now Harvard street, to the top of Corey Hill. His son, Captain John, and grandson Isaac, held the property until it passed into the Griggs family. Elhanan Winchester has been referred to elsewhere in these pages.

The Whites came from John White of Watertown and Brookline, an early and prosperous settler whose will is still preserved in the Public

Library with many other documents relating to the family. He lived in the village. His son, Major Edward White, or Whyte, lived first in a house between Boylston and Washington streets, near their junction, and later on Washington street. He was a wealthy man. Joseph White, brother of Major Edward, lived on the north-eastern corner of Chestnut Hill avenue and Boylston street, before the Ackers family came into possession. Joseph's granddaughter Ann married Henry Sewall, father of Samuel the Tory, and her sister Susanna married Ebenezer Craft, who built the Craft house now standing on the northerly side of Huntington avenue, across the line, with 1709 on the chimney.

The Ackers family, once the leaders in Brookline's rural society, have gone elsewhere. Their farm, about the present Ackers avenue, was once an Indian burying ground.

Among other families were the Buckminsters (mentioned elsewhere), the Druces, the

Davenports, the Heaths, prominent in and since the Revolution, the Kendricks, the Perkinses, and the Cabots ; somewhat later, sturdy Deacon Robinson, the Seavers, from whom came Mayor Seaver of Boston, the Sewalls, the Thayers and the Withingtons.

Before touching upon Brookline's part in the events of the Revolution, the following paragraph from the will of Robert Sharp, dated in 1763, may be of interest as a suggestion of the rural life which prevailed on the eve of the great struggle. It reads : —

"I also give her [my wife] one half of my Poultrey, and honey Bees. . . . I also give her two Cows. . . . I also Give her Twelve Bushell of Indian Corn and Six Bushell of Rie a year Annually so long as She Remains my Widow, And also ten Score of well Fed Pork, and Twelve Score of Good Beef a year Annually And her Firewood at the Door, and so much of the fruit of my Orchard as she wants for her own Use, and six Barrels of Cyder a year Annually. . . . I Further Give her four Bushell of malt a Year Annually. . . . "

To sketch in a rapid way the history of Brookline from the first signs of discontent to the adoption of the constitution, is not an easy task.

In December, 1772, the town chose a committee to take under consideration the violations and infringements of the rights of the colonists. On the 28th they voted : —

"That the Rights of the Colonists, and this Province in particular, as men, as Chrystians & as Subjects, as Set forth in the Votes & Proceedings of the Town of Boston, are in the Opinion of this Town well Stated."

The next month the people went a step further in saying that "this town think themselves happy in being always ready to add their mite to wards withstanding any arbitrary despotick measures that are or may be carried on to overthrow the Constitution and deprive us of all our invaluable rights and priviledges, which are & ought to be as dear or dearer then life itselfe."

In November, 1773, the town voted that they were ready to afford all the assistance in their power to the town of Boston, and would heartily unite with them and the other towns "to oppose and frustrate this most detestable and dangerous tea scheem."

The temper of the people became rapidly hostile to every act of authority exercised by the British crown. In September, 1774, they were bold enough to appoint a committee to examine into the state of the town as to its military preparations for war "in case of a suden attack from our enemies." Upon this committee were John Goddard and Captain Benjamin White, who, with Colonel Thomas Aspinwall and Isaac Gardner, Esq., led the movement which was rapidly drifting toward open rebellion. In the month following the town voted unanimously to approve the measures adopted by the continental congress.

As early as January, 1775, a resort to arms seemed inevitable. John Goddard was busy bringing together military stores under the direction of the committee for supplies. March 8, 1775, according to his note-book, he was carting beef from Boston to Concord. On the 18th he carted two hogsheads of flints and other articles from Boston to Brookline. On the 22d he conveyed sheet lead and three barrels of linen to Concord. On the 24th he carted two casks of leaden balls. On April 10th he carted two ox-cart and two horse-cart loads of canteens to Concord. For some time powder had been concealed at his house near the present Goddard avenue. This was conveyed to Concord, and with the other stores was the cause of the midnight march of Lieutenant-Colonel Smith which brought on the battle of Lexington. Smith had landed at Cambridge, reached Concord, and was retreating when Lord Percy marched to his relief. Word came to Brookline that Lord Percy was coming, and the frightened people gathered together what valuables they could and fled to the upper part of the town. When Lord Percy's one thousand men marched through the village and out Harvard street past Coolidge Corner, he found few of the inhabitants to meet him. The story will always live in Brookline, whether it be true or not, of the small boy who was asked by Lord Percy to point the way to Lexington. His reply was, "You inquire the way there, but I will be damned if you ever need to know the way back."

The first awe which seems to have followed the march of the king's soldiers through the town soon gave place to a desire to fight. By noon almost all of the able-bodied men of the town were gathered on the village green before the meeting-house. From this point, at the corner of Warren and Walnut streets, three

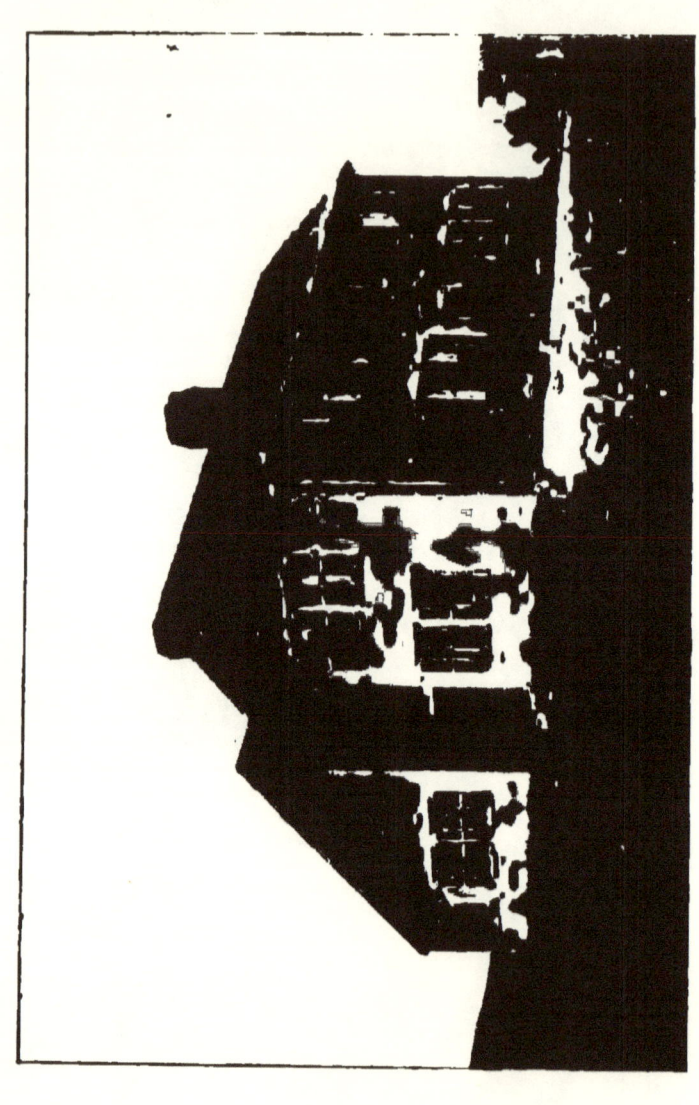

HOUSE OF LIEUTENANT CALEB CRAFT, NEWTON STREET.

Erected by Vincent Druce, between 1660 and 1670.

Vincent Druce's daughter, Bethiah, married Erozomon Drew. His daughter, Ann Drew, married Samuel White. Their daughter, Susannah, married Deacon Ebenezer Craft, who sold the house in 1791 to his son. Caleb Craft.

companies, headed by Captain Thomas White, Colonel Thomas Aspinwall, and Isaac Gardner, Esq., set forth across the fields "as the crow flies" toward Lexington. At half-past two Colonel Smith's exhausted men had been received within a hollow square formed by Lord Percy's reinforcements. At six o'clock the combined forces of the regulars reached Jacob Watson's house near Spruce street, North Cambridge. Here the Brookline volunteers met the British. Isaac Gardner and four or five others posted themselves behind some dry casks near the road. As they waited for Lord Percy to come by on his retreat toward Boston, the enemy's flank guard came behind them and killed every one of them on the spot. Mr. Gardner's body was pierced by balls and bayonets in twelve places. He was the only patriot killed that day who had received a degree from Harvard College.

Dr. Aspinwall, Colonel Aspinwall's brother, calling the Brookline men to follow him, joined in the pursuit of the enemy until at dusk they reached the neighborhood of Charlestown. The doctor was blind in one eye, but was an excellent shot. His friends were not as skillful, for during the running fight that afternoon he was accustomed to place himself on the side of the tree nearest the enemy, preferring to trust to their poor aim rather than to remain too near his excited townsmen.

Dr. Downer, another Brookline volunteer, who did good service in later years as an army surgeon, was active on the 19th of April. While passing a house that afternoon, two British soldiers ran toward him; at that moment one man was shot in the back, while the other exchanged shots with Dr. Downer; although very close to each other they both missed, and the doctor, exasperated, rushed upon the redcoat with his gun and killed him.

Isaac Gardner's body was brought back and buried very quietly the next night. His death caused a bitter but rather amusing controversy in the English press between those who would not believe that His Majesty's Justice of the Peace could have been killed fighting against the crown, and those who, believing the true reports, foresaw the seriousness of the conflict which Great Britain was forcing upon the colonies. The following communication to the *Gazetteer and New Daily Advertiser* of July 4, 1775, copied by Miss Ellen Chase from files in the British Museum, has a spice of the times : —

" Isaac Gardner, one of His Majesty's Justices of the Peace, was not killed as he was *peaceably* riding along, but was killed in the *very act of attacking* the King's troops.

" The rebels in their own accounts, confess this, and confute Mr. Potatoe Head's *falsehoods*. Their account, dated the 24th of April, says that Isaac Gardner took 9 prisoners, that 12 soldiers deserted to him, and that his ambush proved fatal to Lord Percy and another general officer, who were killed the first fire. This is a clear refutation of Mr. Potatoe Head's lying paragraph.

" Mr. Potatoe Head must therefore be, to use one of his own polite epithets, 'a most audacious scoundrel' to impose the *fictions* of his own *Sodden* Head on the public for authentic intelligence from America.

" July 1.   POLITICUS."

During the siege of Boston, Brookline could not well help taking an active interest in the conflict.   John Goddard, as early as the 22d of May, began to be constantly in the service of the province; first, carting stores to the different fortifications which surrounded Boston, and later as far as the Hudson River.   At Sewall's Point, which was on the north-eastern corner of the present Commonwealth avenue extension and Essex street, a fortification was built, mounting six guns, to command the Charles.   Washington once visited it.   On the land in this vicinity, now the Lawrence estate, Colonel Prescott, for a time, had his headquarters, and Colonel Gerrish's regiment and a detachment of the Connecticut troops were stationed.   Their barracks were afterward used as hospitals for the soldiers, much to the annoyance of the people.   Mr. Goddard, Colonel Aspinwall, Captain Corey, Dr. Downer and others of the town's people did loyal service in New England, while Colonel James

GODDARD HOUSE, GODDARD AVENUE.

Built in 1767 by John Goddard.

Wesson, the highest officer from Brookline during the war, was doing gallant service in New York, Pennsylvania and New Jersey. At the battle of Monmouth Court-house in 1778, Colonel Wesson, then in command of the 9th Massachusetts regiment, was in the thickest of the fight. Lying close upon his horse's neck to look under the cannon smoke, he was struck by a ball which tore away his clothing and the muscles of his back. He recovered sufficiently to serve three years longer. In 1784 he moved to Marlboro' and became a prosperous farmer.

But there was always in Brookline a small minority opposed to the patriot cause. A man named Jackson lived near the present Public Library building on Washington street. His house was used as barracks by the American troops, and as a loyal subject of the king, he preferred to sell his property and move away.

Another loyalist was Henry Hulton, mandamus counsellor for the British government. He moved to Boston and the rents of his estate, a portion of which is now the Moses Williams place, were collected by the town until the property was confiscated and sold. The report of a committee, "to the whole court," dated July 2, 1776, "respecting the real & personal estates of those parsons who have fled from us," states: "Wee have taken into our care the farm lately belonging to Henry Hulton, Esq., & have let out for one year to the Rev'd Mr. Jackson & John Coborn of said town, they paying therefore twenty four pounds lawfull money rent." In the list made of his personal estate are: "one suit of curtains, one settee, one matrass bed, two hats, one feather, one sword, two pictures, one chest with about one dazon of glas bottles, one house bell, 11 chana plates, two maps, som sheat led, 1 small bag of brass scruse." The original house was built about 1740 by Nathaniel Gardner, and was owned later by Deacon Benjamin White, and then by Jeremy Gridley, Esq., the distinguished lawyer. Gridley took an active interest in Brookline affairs until the time of his death in 1767. This house, sometimes called the Sumner or Chapin house from more recent owners, was taken down by Mr. Williams in 1885.

Samuel Sewall, although not a resident of Brookline, owned property in the town. He was proscribed as a refugee and sailed for England. Governor Barnard's estate and his pew in the meeting house were, in 1779, ordered sold. But royalists were not the only ones who suffered inconvenience during the war. Major Thompson in a petition to the general court states that on December 14, 1775, Captain King came with an insolent written order to quarter his company in the major's house on the Watertown road. The major protested and stood his ground until the doors were battered in.

Most of the people, however, while the enemy were at their doors were warlike enough, although their inclinations were naturally agricultural rather than military.

In the town records, a vote relating to bounties given by the town to soldiers, stands side by side with the petition of the singing society that they may be allowed to form certain seats in the front gallery of the meeting house into a pew for their better condition.

The following account of farming a place in Roxbury by Robert Sharp and his brother, shows how evenly the farm life continued during ⸝1778 : —

April 22d 1778 my Brother and I agreed to take mothers Place in Roxbury into our hand,—

23d my Brother went over to Roxbury to work with three hands and two teams, I worked with one hand and team.

24th my Brother worked with one hand and Team.

27th my brother Sent one hand and Team. I went with one hand and Sowed five Bushels of Barley and about two quarts of hayseed. my Brother found the Barley and hayseed.

may 16th my Brother sent a hand and Team, I went my Self. we Poled the wall and mended fence.

THE GRIDLEY-HULTON HOUSE, WALNUT STREET,
which stood on the present Moses Williams estate.

From a photograph lent by Moses Williams, Esq.

To face p. 45.

25th my Brother and I went over in the morning. mended fence.

June 1st Each of us turned two Cows into the Pasture.

9th I went over in the after noon with my Brothers hand and Team. Sowed half a Bushel of Flax Seed which I gave two Dollars for the Flax Seed.

July 20th we went to mowing Robert three hands in the fore noon two in the afternoon I one hand all day. Robert found a leg of bacon and Sauce. I found two gallons of Cyder, one Gallon of rum, cheese &c.

21t Robert had five hands a mowing all day, two hand rakeing in the afternoon I had one hand mowing, Robert found two quarts of rum a quarter mutton Sauce &c. I found pork &c.

22d I Stayed with four of Roberts hands and one of my own and raked till towards night.

24th. I went with Thomas and aaron in the after noon and raked meadowhay.

25th Robert went with a team and four hands. I with a team and two hands we Carted hay into the barn. I found a small quarter of lamb Cheese etc.

29th Robert went with a team and two hands I with a team and one hand we mowed and Carted home the Barley. I found a gallon rum Cheese &c.

August 25 I went with my team thomas & Aaron pul'd the Flax brouht it to Jamaca pond.

With the return to agriculture which followed the transfer of the seat of war to New York came an aversion to joining the continentals. In 1779 a committee was appointed to hire the number of men which the town was called upon to raise to reinforce the continental army. After several discouraging attempts to get volunteers, the town voted, July 13, 1780 :—

"That Capt. White be desired to Issue his Warrant to warn the Training Band and alarm list to meet to Morrow afternoon at five a Clock in this place in order to raise the Remainder of the Town's Quota of Men by draft if they cannot be Raised any other way be fore that time; and that Notice be given that such persons as shall not attend the meeting, be the first Drafted."

At the next meeting it was voted that Doctor Aspinwall and Deacon Gardner "go around among the people in the present meeting to see who will advance money for the purpose of hiring men," and "to go around among the people present to see if any incline to ingage to serve as soldiers for the town."

The regular committee refused to serve, and a new committee was appointed with instructions not to give more than £1500 per man for the militia, which were called for three months. There can be no doubt that the people present were slow to "ingage to serve as soldiers for the town."

As there are in the Public Library many receipts for fine-money received from prominent citizens who refused to join the army when drafted, the form of these may still be of interest : —

BROOKLINE, Decr. ye 9th 1776.

Recd of Mr. Caleb Craft the Sum of Ten Pounds Lawfull money in full for his fine he Refuseing to go a Solder when Draughted by the Town.

Reced by me THOS. ASPINWALL.

Miss Mary Boylston in 1780 hoped to awaken some enthusiasm by her offer of three silver dollars, given "for the encouragement of such men as shall ingage to serve as soldiers." It would perhaps be unkind to mention that she failed to pay her taxes that very year.

In January, 1781, it was voted "that every inhabitant be authorized to hire any soldiers to serve for three years, or during the war for this town's quota for the continental army—and that every inhabitant that shall procure a man shall be allowed four dollars for his trouble."

Still later, in July, the town was divided into eight classes in order to procure eight men to go to Rhode Island and West Point. Each class was obliged to procure one man and pay him. Any class that failed to fulfill this obligation was to pay the highest price given for any of the men. The following receipt relates to this period :—

BROOKLINE August 21st 1782.
Recd of Robert Sharp by the hand of Col. Wesson, Eight Pounds 2/ in full for his part for hiring a Soldier for three years, for the fourth Class in the Town of Brookline.

8:5:9¾   DANIEL WHITE.

The calls for troops ceased toward the end of the war, and the patriotism which may have been dampened by the frequent demands for reinforcements, grew brighter. In September, 1782, came the last call for men. The war was soon ended, and the farmers were no longer interrupted in their agricultural pursuits.

Soon after this, the wealthier people of Boston began to look toward Brookline, with its beautiful woodlands, as a desirable place for country homes. This movement in the last one hundred years has changed the town from a community too poor to send a representative, to one so wealthy that it is in danger of becoming a prey to its avaricious neighbors.

The population of Brookline in 1700 was probably not far from 300. In 1800 it had risen to 605. Forty years later, there were 1265 people in the town. Fifty-five years from that time the town had 15,000 people, with an estimated annual increase of over 1000 people. The chief event at the opening of the nineteenth century was the dedication of a new meeting house, June 11, 1806. Then, and for many years after, this was the town's property, and Dr. Pierce was the spiritual leader of all the people. The next day began the demolition of the little church where the fathers had worshipped since 1717. On the site of this second church now stands the Unitarian church erected in 1893. On the other side of Walnut street, at the bend, the house once owned by Henry Hulton remained until 1885. Before Mr. Hulton came to Brookline to live, the house was occupied by Jeremy Gridley, Esq., attorney general for the king, and sometimes called " the Webster of his time." In the famous trial before Chief Justice Hutchinson, when James Otis attempted to show that the writs of assistance were unconstitutional, Mr. Gridley upheld the Crown. During a speech of four hours in length, called by Adams the " birth of liberty," Otis treated Gridley with marked respect and courtesy.

Another famous character in Brookline history, at a little later time, was Miss Hannah Adams, the first woman in America who made literature a profession. She was the author of a History of the Jews, a History of New England, Letters on the Gospels, a View of Religious Opinions, etc. Dr. Pierce says of her : " She was as notorious for ignorance of common household concerns, and indeed of common things in general, as she was celebrated for book-learning, and eminent for piety."

During the same period, the Hon. George Cabot, United States senator, and secretary of the navy under Adams, came to Brookline, and also Hon. Jonathan Mason, United States senator.

Brookline, like all New England, took little interest in the war of 1812, except in self-defence. Mr. A. W. Goddard remembers seeing from Goddard Heights the Chesapeake sail down Boston harbor, June 1, 1813, to fight the Shannon. In the autumn of 1814, fearing the arrival of a British fleet, the militia poured into Boston to man the forts in the harbor. At this time a number of citizens organized a company of about fifty men to serve in case of invasion. The officers were General Isaac S. Gardner, captain ; Major John Robinson, lieutenant ; and Joseph Goddard, ensign. Many of the people volunteered in November to work in the fortifications then being thrown up on the heights of South Boston, and on Noddle's Island. Later a company was organized for service at Fort Inde-

THE BABCOCK-GODDARD HOUSE, WARREN STREET.

Built by Nehemiah Davis.

Owned later by Hon. George Cabot, Stephen Higginson, Jr., Adam Babcock, and Samuel Goddard.

From a photograph lent by Miss Julia Goddard.

To face p. 55.

pendence, with Timothy Corey, captain, Robert
S. Davis, lieutenant, and Thomas Griggs, ensign.
The citizens raised a contribution to be divided
among them. During the splendid defence of
Fort Erie, near Buffalo, August 15, 1814, where
General Drummond after a brave assault was
driven back, the right was held by General
Scott's brigade commanded by Lieutenant-
Colonel Thomas Aspinwall of Brookline. In an
attack on the British lines, September 17, Aspin-
wall lost his left arm while directing his men
within twenty paces of the enemy's defences.

An event in the social history of the town
may be chronicled here. The Marquis de
Lafayette while visiting the United States dined
with Colonel T. H. Perkins June 20, 1825. Upon
taking leave of his host the marquis rode along
Heath street, which was lined by spectators. He
stopped before the home of Ebenezer Heath, and
shook hands with every young lady present. Miss
Elizabeth P. Peabody, then a girl of twenty-one,

mounted the steps of the carriage and kissed his hand. For many years Miss Peabody always appeared at tea time on the anniversary of this day to celebrate the event in the company of the Misses Anne and Susan Heath.

In 1806–7 the present Boylston street, from the village over Bradley's Hill to the Reservoir, and from Heath street westward, was built. As a turnpike road to Worcester, it went over hill and through dale, regardless of the comfort of teamsters. It seems to have had no more effect upon the development of Brookline than did the old route through Walnut street and Heath street, for the large estates on Heath, Warren, Clyde and Boylston streets have never been invaded by the allotment promoter.

At first the mill-dam from " Charles street in Boston across the bay and over Brookline marshes to Sewall's point," built in 1821, had little influence on the town, for the toll of 6¼ cents hindered travel.

The laying out of Beacon street and the construction of a branch railroad into the town — perhaps the two greatest events in Brookline history during the first half of this century — were bitterly opposed. The Boston and Worcester railroad had been opened as far as Newton in 1834. In 1846 a committee was instructed to assist counsel "at every stage of the business in and out of the legislature to show the ruinous consequence" of allowing a railroad to pass through the village.

On the 8th of April, 1848, the Brookline branch railroad was opened to the public. "S. A. W." in the *Boston Daily Journal*, Wednesday, April 12th, writes : —

"Never shone the sun more effulgent, never did the countenances of the inhabitants of Brookline bespeak more joy, than on the day appointed for the opening of the grand project of Railroad communication with the city. On Saturday last, by the liberality of the Directors of the Boston and Worcester Railroad, more than 2000 persons, mostly inhabitants of Brookline and vicinity, passed over this delightful avenue, and notwithstanding there were *fourteen* trains that passed to and from the city during the day, not the slightest accident occurred.

"At the appointed time, the long train of cars drawn by the 'Iron Horse,' decked with the American ensign, was signalized from the bend at the entrance to the town, and was welcomed at the depot, amid the thundering of cannon and the ringing of bells, while the long continued and deafening cheers of the multitude bespoke the grateful prompting of their hearts."

Regular trains began to run April 10th. The first time-table in the Boston papers reads : —

BOSTON AND WORCESTER RAILROAD.
BROOKLINE SPECIAL TRAINS.

Leave Brookline at 8, 9 and 11 A. M., 2, 3½, 6 and 7½ P. M.
Leave Boston at 8½ and 10 A. M., 12¼, 2½, 4½, 7 and 9½ P. M.

All baggage at the risk of its owner. Fares are less when paid at the ticket offices than when paid in the cars.

BOSTON, April 5, 1848.   WM. PARKER, Sup't.

In 1849 "after a protracted discussion" a vote was passed "by a very large majority" to appoint a committee to oppose the construction of a public road "from the northern end of the Mill-Dam road westerly through this town to Brighton line" by "every lawful and proper means, and employ counsel if they deem it necessary."

FIRST LOCOMOTIVE TO RUN ON THE BROOKLINE BRANCH RAILROAD.

From a picture given to the Public Library by Dr. T. F. Francis, November 22, 1894.

The locomotive "Lion," afterwards "Brookline, and still later the "Farmingdale," was built at the Bury Works, Liverpool, in the year 1835. During the 32 years she was in use by the Boston and Worcester Railroad, she ran over 700,000 miles, or more than any other locomotive in the United States. Her weight was twelve tons, and she was formerly without cab or truck-wheels.

The section of this road west of Washington street was laid out in 1850, and the connection with the mill-dam in 1851, the two parts forming Beacon street. In 1886-7 this road was made into a parkway, 160 to 180 feet in width. Of the entire cost, $615,000, the town paid $465,000. In six years the land and buildings for five hundred feet on either side in Brookline increased in assessed values $4,330,400, or more than 500 per cent. The Telford macadam construction is used in the road-bed, and costs, including watering and the cutting of the grass, about $6,000 a year to maintain.

The special provision for street cars on the Beacon street boulevard offered an opportunity to introduce rapid transit by electric cars. Electricity had been tried in the South in an almost primitive way, and success in Brookline after repeated and costly experiments, developed - the first successful electric street railway in the world.

The leading spirit in this movement was Mr.
Henry M. Whitney, at about that time president
of the West End Land Company, and of the
West End Street Railway.   Mr. Whitney is a
son of the late General Whitney of the town,
and a brother of the Hon. William C. Whitney
of New York, ex-secretary of the navy.

An active friend of the measure was the Hon.
William Aspinwall, a leader in the town meetings of Brookline for half a century, town
clerk, selectman, assessor, state representative
and senator, and trustee of the Public Library
until his death in 1892.   Mr. Aspinwall was a
whig and later a democrat.   He always had a
substantial following in spite of his very forcible
way of putting things.

A horse car line, running from each end of
School street through the village by the ancient
route of travel to Roxbury Crossing, was opened
about 1858.   Later, tracks were laid through
Longwood avenue to Coolidge Corner.

The civil war awakened a very different spirit in Brookline from that aroused by the war of 1812. The bombardment of Fort Sumter, April 12, 1861, and the attack upon a Massachusetts regiment in the streets of Baltimore April 19th, made the war seem unavoidable. While the preservation of the Union was the first rallying cry, long years of slave hunting in Boston and of slave harboring in Brookline, especially at the Philbrick house on Walnut street, then a station on the "underground railway," had developed an uncompromising attitude toward this distinguishing institution of the South.

At a meeting held in Brookline April 20, 1861, the presiding officer, John Howe, offered to transfer a land-warrant received for services in the war of 1812 to the family who first lost a husband or father in the struggle. Subscription

lists were opened and George B. Blake offered
$1000. At the same meeting Wilder Dwight
suggested the organization of one or more companies. On the 22d, the following citizens were
chosen to serve the town as a military committee for one year: Moses B. Williams, chairman, James A. Dupee, Marshall Stearns, William
K. Melcher, Nathaniel Lyford, Thomas B. Hall,
Thomas Parsons, William Aspinwall, James
Murray Howe and Edward A. Wild.

During the two years in which this committee
served, Dr. Hall resigned, and James Bartlett
took Mr. Wild's place. Thereafter the selectmen carried on the work.

The first soldier to enlist, April 23d, was
William D. Goddard, a grandson of William
Dawes, the revolutionary patriot. On the 28th
of April, Simon Cameron, secretary of war,
authorized Wilder Dwight of Brookline and
George L. Andrews to raise a regiment in
Massachusetts for service during the war. Mr.

BEACON STREET, BEFORE THE WIDENING.

Looking west toward Coolidge Corner.

From a photograph lent by Charles H. Stearns, Esq.

Dwight became major of the 2d regiment of infantry in May. His enthusiasm, untiring energy and ability, promised a distinguished career. In the regiment's first action he was captured, and after being exchanged returned to his post. He was mortally wounded at the battle of Antietam and lay all night under the fire of both armies. His death occurred a few days later in a house near the battlefield. A fine portrait of Major Dwight by Eastman Johnson hangs in the Public Library.

The town hired a hall in the Guild block at the corner of Boylston and Washington streets, and recruiting and drilling began. In May Edward A. Wild received a commission as captain of a new company, with William L. Candler and Charles L. Chandler as lieutenants, and on May 25, 1861, Colonel Harrington of Brookline mustered them into the United States service as Company A of the 1st Massachusetts volunteer infantry.

Captain (later Brigadier General) Wild was born in Brookline, November 25, 1825, the son of Dr. Charles Wild. After graduating at Harvard and the Jefferson Medical College of Philadelphia he began to practice. While traveling in Europe some time after this he took too much interest in Garibaldi's campaign and was arrested. In 1855 he was married, and at once set out for Turkey, where his services as surgeon were accepted for the Crimean war. General Wild served through the civil war, was mustered out January 15, 1866, and died at Medellin, Colombia, August 28, 1891.

Lieutenant Candler was the son of Captain John Candler of the navy, and a brother of the Hon. John W. Candler of Brookline, at one time a member of congress. He rose rapidly during the war, and at its close engaged in mining until his death in 1893.

Lieutenant Chandler was the son of Theophilus P. Chandler of Brookline, and a brother of Alfred D. Chandler, Esq. ; their sister married Lieutenant Candler in 1862. March 6, 1864, Chandler was commissioned lieutenant-colonel of the 57th regiment, which he commanded at the battle of the Wilderness, and until his death, May 24, 1864, from wounds received at North Anna River.

On the 15th of June the 1st regiment, of which Company A formed a part, started for the front, the first three years' regiment to reach Washington. The town had provided generously for the company, and the women had made clothing for each man's comfort. Among the volunteers was Herbert Barlow of Brookline, a kinsman of General Francis Barlow. His letters, with one by General Wild, throw a glow of life into the events of the first year's service of the company. They are the letters of one hardly more than a boy, and their unaffected language gives a picture not to be found in any official records. The first letter dated at Washington, June 18, 1861, tells how he "walked over to Cambridge and got there just in time to catch the horse-cars, getting to the camp about seven o'clock." In the course of the forenoon they had their haversacks, canteens, etc., given to them, together with four days' rations of hard bread and ham. In the afternoon they marched to Boston, took the train to Groton and went by boat to Jersey City. They marched through Baltimore "with fixed bayonets and loaded muskets," and in course of time arrived at their quarters in Pennsylvania avenue in Washington, "gloriously tired and hungry." In the second letter he relates : " I was walking up and down my beat, thinking of home, when I saw two horsemen coming out of the camp. Down came my gun to the charge, and stopped them with 'Who goes there?' They answered 'Grand round,' and after giving the countersign, which was 'Maine,' passed on. A few minutes after another man came up who proved to be the colonel, and said : ' I am glad you stopped those fellows. I wouldn't have had them get by you without being challenged for a good deal.' "

A short note written in pencil and dated " In the woods near Centreville, Va., July 19, 1861," begins " Dear Mother : We had a pretty hard fight yesterday, near Manassas Junction, our company being in the thickest of the fire. Had to retreat, as the enemy was too strong for us. We are however marching forward again today, and shall probably have hot work before night." With what anxiety must a mother have awaited news after such a letter !

The next letter is dated " Camp Banks, July 23d, 1861." After describing the march to Bull Run where they met the enemy, he continues : —

"We formed in a deep gully and marched steadily up the hill, on the top of which the enemy were posted in large numbers ; after one or two fires we were compelled to retreat, but formed again in the gully, and deployed as skirmishers. Then each man had to look out for himself

and I went dodging along behind the trees, close beside
Captain Adams. While I stood near him a rifle ball
struck a tree between us, knocking off a piece of bark
which hit him in the eye, blacking it all round. Our
forces had posted two pieces of artillery on the edge of
the woods to support us, but the rebels kept up such a
fire that they retreated, leaving one gun behind them.
Our captain called up a lot of us boys and ordered us to
fire into the woods over the cannon, which we did till the
gunners came back and hitching on their horses retreated
in safety. The fire of the rebels in the meanwhile was
so galling that we again retreated to the gully. Lieutenant-Colonel Wells then asked for volunteers to go up and
bring down the wounded, when our whole company said
they would go, but the moment we showed our heads over
the hill, the enemy poured in volley after volley upon us
till the officers said it was madness to go further, so we
retreated from the woods covered by the 2d Michigans.
Then we went over the hill behind our artillery, which
kept up a fire until nearly dark, when the whole brigade
retreated about a mile, when we laid on our guns all
night. The next morning I sent a bit of a note to you
by a gentleman who was going to Boston. which I sup-
pose you got. We stayed in the woods until Sunday,
when we had another battle, our regiment having the
post of honor, which was covering the artillery. We had
no fighting, however and were the last to leave the field.
The division on the right of us had a terrible fight and
was cut all to pieces. The N. Y. Fire Zouaves have only
four hundred left, and the Massachusetts Fifth lost so

many that they could not march over their dead. We had an hour's sleep and then commenced our retreat, marching nearly forty miles from twelve o'clock Sunday night to yesterday afternoon, about 14 hours. When we got to Camp Banks we were almost dead with fatigue and wet through with rain. Some hundred or two men fell down with fatigue on the road, and have not yet got into camp. Will Conway is well. The exact number of killed and wounded I don't know, but you will probably see it in the papers. It is reported that we march to Arlington Heights this afternoon, but I don't know how true it is. On our retreat we had nothing to eat, our last rations having been dealt out Sunday morning; so when we got into camp last night the coffee and bread the sick ones had ready for us, disappeared like magic.

"Love to Anna.

HERBERT."

The next letter is dated at Arlington, Va., July 25, 1861.

"*Dear Mother :*—Yesterday that box of yours arrived in safety, after laying in the express office in Georgetown nearly a week. You know it got there just after I left 'for the war.'

"In my last letter I was too tired to write much of an account about our fights, though I did write something about the first one, which took place last Thursday. On Sunday we had another one, but our regiment was posted in the woods to support the artillery, and so could not see much. It appears, however, that the division on our right was badly whipped, for we retreated all night, marching over thirty-five miles in fourteen hours, and when you recollect that we have big heavy shoes on our feet, a gun on our shoulder, two blankets (rubber and woolen) on our back, together with a haversack and canteen, you will see that is anything but play. All along the road we saw wagons tipped over and abandoned, which was a perfect godsend to us poor fellows, for we had had no rations delivered to us since Saturday morning, and in the wagons were plenty of good crackers, which you may be sure we pitched into with a will.

"Captain Wild is now as popular among us as he was unpopular before, he having behaved like a brick all through the fight, handling a musket and fighting like a tiger.

"It is all very well for anyone in Massachusetts to run down our colonel while we are away, but after the 'gallant first' gets home, whoever speaks against him will be in danger of being knocked down. Anyone who doubts his bravery should have seen him when the cannons were playing upon us, and they would change their minds.

"You ask me 'if I don't wish I was at home again.' *That I do!* I've had enough of soldiering, and would give 'all my boots and shoes' for an honorable discharge. Not that I care for the *fighting*, but the marches I can't stand.

"This afternoon we march to Fort Albany, about two miles from here, nearer Washington, where we shall probably stay awhile.

WASHINGTON STREET BRIDGE, APRIL 17, 1885.

From a picture owned by the town.

" I wish you would make two or three strips of tape

H. S. Barlow,

Co. F, First Regiment Mass. Volunteers,

and send them in your next letter. All the letters which had come to Camp Banks while we were away, were sent to us to Bull's Run, and were brought up to us while we were in the woods during the progress of the fight on Sunday. You would have been amused to have seen us fellows standing and laying around with our guns at our sides, reading a word or two, and then looking across the field to see if the enemy were making any movement; the cannons thundering away and the air full of smoke.

" We did n't any of us know but what it might be the last time we should ever hear from home, and, therefore, devoured every word.

" Cliff thanks Tom for his present.

HERBERT.

" Direct as usual. H. W. B."

In a letter from Camp Union, October 10, 1861, he describes the rebel flag taken some days before: "The stars are five pointed, nine in number, arranged in a circle of eight with one in the center."

A few words at the end of a letter from Budd's Ferry, dated Nov. 15, 1861, show the solicitude that many mothers must have felt at the

announcements from time to time in the daily
papers, of soldiers shot for falling asleep while
on picket duty.

General Wild in a letter dated at Camp
Hooker, Budd's Ferry, Nov. 26, 1861, sent to the
war committee a grateful acknowledgment of
shirts, stockings, mittens, etc., made by the
ladies of the First Parish.   He then told how on
November 14, 1861, a schooner attempted to
pass up the Potomac, but was becalmed within
range of the rebel batteries.   The crew, who had
been under constant fire for most of the forenoon, abandoned her, and the rebels soon rowed
a boat out and went on board.   Lieutenant
Candler, who was watching the enemy, sent a
messenger on horseback three miles down the
shore to the camp.   Captain Wild, officer of the
day, at once ordered Company A under Lieutenant Chandler to the landing place.   Thirty-three
men all told put off in the largest boat with
Wild and Chandler, and after a pull of three miles

came alongside the schooner which was already in flames. She was loaded with firewood, and although the men expected an explosion at any moment they, by the greatest exertion, threw the deckload overboard and extinguished the fire. During this time the enemy sent eighty-three shots through the rigging and into the water. At last the anchor was hoisted, the jib and flying jib set, and she was worked up the river out of range. "Company A," wrote their captain, "behaved admirably ; perfectly steady."

Of the 667 men of proper age in Brookline, only 378 were declared suitable for service at the front. Companies of volunteers were formed for daily drill on the Town Hall grounds. Two field pieces were procured, and the men who perfected themselves in the use of these almost all became members in September, 1861, of the 10th Massachusetts battery.

Meanwhile, the boys between the ages of twelve and fifteen organized the Brookline Rifles, and became so proficient that they were asked to give exhibitions in other towns. The girls carried linen to school, and during recess picked lint to be sent to the hospitals.

On the 31st of January, 1862, Herbert Barlow was accidentally shot, and was brought home and buried with military honors. News came late one Saturday night in August of the second battle of Bull Run, and the loss of the hospital stores. Mr. George B. Blake at once notified all the ministers, and Sunday morning the congregations were dismissed to prepare bandages and supplies to be sent south. Hon. Ginery Twitchell, president of the Boston & Worcester railroad, lived on Kent street at this time. He immediately telegraphed for cars and engines to carry goods and surgeons to Washington. Two loaded freight cars were sent in from Brookline before sundown, and these with eight from Boston reached Washington early Tuesday morning. Mr. Twitchell, Dr. Tappan E. Francis

THE COREY-SEARS HOMESTEAD, WASHINGTON STREET.

Torn down in 1897.

and others went with the train. When Mr. Twitchell returned, a meeting was held in the Baptist church, at which he read a letter from President Lincoln to the people of Brookline.

Years afterward, Mr. Twitchell entertained in Brookline the great military leader of the war, General U. S. Grant. The general walked into the fields east of Kent street to see some wild animals kept by Mr. Twitchell's son.

Through 1863, 1864 and 1865, patriotic meetings were held and the work of recruiting went on systematically. At the meetings patriotic speeches were made by prominent officers from different parts of the country, and by soldiers home on furlough, or by Moses B. Williams, William Aspinwall, Amos A. Lawrence, J. Murray Howe, William A. Wellman, Mr. Blake, W. Y. Gross, Ginery Twitchell, Thomas Parsons and other citizens. Between the speeches the band played popular music. Mr. Williams, Mr. Howe,

Edward Atkinson and many others pledged large sums of money.

The names of those who came forward and enlisted would fill many pages, and it seems unjust to single out any for mention in so short a sketch. Their names are recorded at the end of this book, where will be found also the names of many of the present citizens (1897), who served in the army or navy before they came to Brookline.

In New York, Colonel Frank Howe, a Brookline man doing business there, opened his store to the sick and wounded Massachusetts soldiers, who were being helped on their way toward the North. He not only raised funds for this object, but also helped to keep up the spirits of the supporters of the government.

When at last the news came that the war was over, the church bells were rung throughout the town, and the houses were trimmed with bunting. Brookline had furnished 720 men, over one hundred more than had been demanded. Of these about one-third were citizens of the town. Of the whole number enlisted, seventy-two were killed. The town spent during the war the sum of $134,244.99, and the women are said to have spent an additional $20,000 in their work.

In looking at Brookline on the map, two facts are worthy of notice; first, that the town, which has been a part of Norfolk county since 1793, is entirely separated from the rest of the county, as is the case in certain parts of England; and secondly, that Boston almost surrounds the town. As Brookline has wealth, two results were inevitable, a desire on the part of Boston to annex the smaller neighbor, and a determination on the part of Norfolk county not to lose so valuable a territory. How powerful these forces are may be estimated from the figures so ably presented by Alfred D. Chandler, Esq., in a pamphlet entitled, "Brookline, a Study in Town Government." The metropolitan district of Boston within a radius of about ten miles of the Brookline Town Hall, contains a million people. From 1882 to 1892 this district gained in assessed

B. F. Baker

From a photograph taken in 1892,
his fortieth year of service as town clerk.

To face p. 77.

valuation over $353,000,000. During this time Chicago, perhaps the most wonderful example of the growth of a modern city, gained but $118,373,601, in assessed valuation, or less than one-half, while the greater population was at this time in Chicago.

In 1870 an unsuccessful attempt was made to annex "towns and parts of towns lying within six miles of the City Hall of the city of Boston on the southerly side of Charles River." Two years later some Brookline citizens petitioned for annexation and the matter came up again. The arguments advanced by Hamilton A. Hill, and approved by a majority of the commission appointed by the mayor of Boston in 1872, have in great measure lost what force they once had. Brookline now has the broad streets leading to Boston, which he thought annexation would bring. The problems of water supply and sewage are being solved by metropolitan commissions. His best argument was, however, that

Brighton, since the slaughter-houses were better managed, should be improved in connection with the adjacent territory " on a broad and comprehensive plan " that " its many picturesque situations" might " attract a large number of people." This yoke Brookline was to bear.

On May 16, 1873, an act was passed to annex Brookline to Boston, to take effect if a majority of the voters, on the first Tuesday of October, 1873, signified their approval. Thirteen days later a bill in equity was filed by T. P. Chandler, Augustus Lowell, Ignatius Sargent, John L. Gardner, Amos A. Lawrence, Robert Amory, T. E. Francis, James S. Amory, John C. Abbott and Isaac Taylor, all of Brookline, to restrain Boston and Brookline from proceeding under this act. June 24th, A. D. Chandler, Esq., presented an argument for the bill, on the ground that "the citizens of the town of Brookline had and have the right to a popular form of municipal government, guaranteed to them by the constitution of Massachusetts, and that as the annexation of Brookline to the city of Boston would subject them to a representative form of government, this guaranteed right would be lost and the constitution be violated."

The court did not take this view of the case, and the popular vote on October 7th saved the town. This vote of 707 to 299 was the result of hard work as well as good judgment. The advocates of annexation persisted in the fight, saying there was a ring at the Town Hall, and that town government was a failure.

The following extract from the annual report of the selectmen, March, 1874, was probably written by the chairman, Mr. Charles D. Head :—

"The town is once more called on to defend itself from being absorbed — a worse fate than befell the prophet Jonah, for he was swallowed singly, while if we go down we shall find previous competitors for internal advantages, and if dissatisfied with the want of accommodation, or if we disagree with our hospitable host, we shall not be likely to recover our liberty, or identity, as he did."

In 1875, 1876 and 1879 unsuccessful attempts were made. In October, 1879, the last serious struggle began. The petition in favor of annexation, dated October 20, 1879, bore 333 names. Mr. Chandler, in his argument for Brookline before the committee on towns of the legislature, states that these represented about seven per cent of the valuation of the town. Eight names on the list appeared twice, 210 only represented legal voters and 74 did not appear on the voting or property lists of the town. A test vote was taken in the spring, which resulted in 541 votes against annexation and 272 votes in its favor. The committee on towns heard all sides, including the protest of Norfolk county, and their report against annexation was accepted by the legislature. Mr. Chandler, in reply to those who claimed that men who do business in Boston should vote there, said: "It is apparent that the great fortunes of the heavy tax-payers of Brookline have been made largely outside of Boston, and not within it, otherwise Boston would not only be the hub but the whole of the universe. The world at large, all parts of which have paid tribute to Boston merchants, would ridicule the monstrous conceit which attributed to Boston itself the fortunes its merchants have made."

West Roxbury and Brighton were annexed to Boston in 1873. In 1880 the valuation of the former alone exceeded that of Brookline. In 1893, although the area of the two towns was more than double that of Brookline, the valuation of Brookline exceeded that of West Roxbury and Brighton combined.

In November, 1894, the metropolitan park commission had a hearing in the Town Hall to ascertain public opinion in regard to placing the parks, sewers, schools, police, etc., of Boston and the neighboring towns under one government, or to annex the towns. Brookline favored some form of metropolitan system with limited powers. But the interest was slight and the matter was dropped.

THE LAST QUARTER OF THE NINETEENTH CENTURY.

Of three streams which influence the topography of Brookline, one—Smelt brook—running close to Judge Sewall's three farms, Brooklin, Swamplin and Hogs-coat, gave the town its name ; another— the Village brook — now disappearing in a culvert, guided the course of the village railroad ; and Muddy river, which gave Brookline its earliest designation, is the origin of a parkway.

In the earliest days sailing vessels came up Muddy river as far as the present Longwood avenue bridge to the oyster beds, and later to the brick and lumber yards. When the mill-dam was built in 1821 this traffic was cut off. March 30, 1880, the subject of the " Improvement of Muddy river" was referred to a committee, consisting of the selectmen and three park commissioners elected at the same meeting. These commissioners, F. W. Lawrence, Theodore Lyman and Charles S. Sargent, presented a plan, prepared by Mr. Frederick Law Olmsted of Brookline, for a "continuous promenade" extending from the Common through Commonwealth avenue, and through grounds laid out on either side of Muddy river to Jamaica pond. The plan was printed in colors in the town report for 1881. Part of the land to be acquired lay in Boston and part in Brookline. Delays were occasioned by the fact that Boston had reached her debt limit, and by the high prices asked by some of the land owners. The work went steadily on, however, and as early as 1883 the new improvement was called Riverdale park. In 1895 the commissioners reported that the work of construction was substantially finished. The total cost of the park, including maintenance, less the amount received for betterments, was $457,069.97. Thus the marshes of ancient

THE BROOKLINE PUBLIC BATH, TAPPAN STREET.

From a sketch lent by Dr. H. Lincoln Chase.

To face p. 85.

Muddy river have been transformed into a beautiful parkway of drives and walks, grassy mounds, shrubs and trees.

Brookline was a part of Suffolk county until June 20, 1793, when the act of March 26th, to set off Norfolk county (second of the name) took effect. Brookline became a part of the new county, and still holds this relation, although through the encroachments of Boston on the surrounding territory the town has been entirely separated from Dedham, the county seat. The new court-house at Dedham was dedicated June 20, 1895, and a handsome memorial of the occasion has been published. The county commissioners were charged with extravagance, and as Brookline pays about thirty-five per cent of the total Norfolk county tax, the town took a leading part in the investigations.

In 1880 there was an unsuccessful attempt to erect and maintain a public bath-house under the acts of 1874. On April 18, 1883, an appropriation of $3,000 was made for " one or more public bath-houses." In 1890 Robert Bishop, chairman of a committee on free warm baths, recommended a bath-house and swimming-tank, to be erected on Tappan street, but the plan was given up. In April, 1895, the subject of improved bathing facilities came up in town meeting, and was referred to a committee consisting of Dr. H. Lincoln Chase, Mr. James B. Hand, and Miss Martha W. Edgerly. On October 24th, after some discussion, the town voted to have a new public bath at a cost of $25,000. The building committee was to include the former committee and the board of selectmen. January 30, 1896, the cost of construction was allowed to be $40,000, exclusive of the land on the southern side of Tappan street and of furnishing. The bath-house was finished in December, 1896. Under the general direction of Dr. Chase, whose knowledge of the subject and unceasing activity were invaluable to the town, aided by an efficient committee, a building has been constructed with rain baths, tubs, a tank eighty feet by twenty-six feet, lined with English white-glazed brick, a tank twenty-two feet by ten feet, about fifty dressing-rooms with front and rear entrances, a gallery or running track, toilet rooms, and a small laundry for towels and trunks. The architect, Mr. F. Joseph Untersee of Brookline, has planned one of the few public buildings architecturally creditable to the town. The construction was intrusted to King & Hodge, Kenrick Brothers, Mr. John F. Fleming, and other Brookline contractors. The inscription cut in stone over the entrance reads :—

THE HEALTH OF THE PEOPLE
THE BEGINNING OF HAPPINESS.

The interior is brightened by lettering on the walls : the vote in town meeting, quotations from the poets, and the names of famous swimmers, Ulysses, Leander, Thermuthis, Horatius,

Cæsar, Charlemagne, Olaf Trygvesson, Nicolo
of Cola, Wynman, Franklin, Von Pfuel, Webb.
The dedicatory exercises took place January 1,
1897.

At the close of the nineteenth century increase
in population about the old centers of growth
has become less marked; while new centers,
like Mr. Knapp's beautiful Beaconsfield terraces
at the northerly end of Tappan street, Mr.
McKay's Babcock farm allotment, and the allot-
ments near Chestnut Hill station are attracting
the seekers for homes. If Brookline is favored
in the character of those who come, it is largely
due to efficient administration of town affairs.
At the town meetings, where every citizen has
a voice, town officers are elected, appropriations
are made, and projects are discussed. With a
population large enough to entitle Brookline to
a city charter, the necessarily large volume of
business is transacted quickly and safely at town
meetings because the "Committee of twenty"

GREEN HILL, WARREN STREET.

The estate of John L. Gardner, Esq.

(appointed by the moderator at the annual town meeting) examines and comments in a printed report upon each subject to be brought before the people. This report and the annual town report insure publicity.

The magnitude of the interests involved may be inferred from a synopsis of the report of the town treasurer, Mr. George H. Worthley, for the year ending February 15, 1897:—

Treasury receipts from all sources . . .	$1,640,077 81
Total payments	1,596,410 37
Cash on hand	$43,667 44
Entire debt (including $727,172 for water)	$2,079,212 00
Sinking fund securities (at par) and cash	$491,982 03
Assessed value of real estate	$45,802,600 00
Assessed value of personal estate . . .	15,194,200 00
Total valuation	$60,996,800 00
Tax rate	$12.40 per $1000
Population, estimated	17.000
Polls assessed	4.562

If there is some local pride in Brookline, has it sprung from unworthy sources? Is it not the pride that comes from an inheritance well administered, a beautiful home-spot made more beautiful by industry and temperance? As Brookline has emulated the good in other communities, may not other towns profit by that loyalty and that public spirit which characterize every good citizen within its borders?

It should be said that this narrative of particular events in Brookline history does not mention adequately some who have been most closely associated with the progress of the town : Horace James, chairman of the board of selectmen; Benjamin F. Baker, town clerk ; William H. Lincoln, chairman, and William T. R. Marvin, secretary, of the school committee.

BROOKLINE IN LITERATURE AND THE ARTS.

In these days the name of Brookline is associated with the possession of wealth. Yet throughout the town's history literature has been represented in a degree somewhat unusual outside of a college town. The beginnings of Brookline are linked with two names eminent in early history. Governor John Winthrop was the first writer to mention the town. In his Journal he records that in 1632 "notice being given of ten Sagamores and many Indians being assembled at Muddy River, the Governor sent Captain Underhill with twenty musketeers to make discoveries, but at Roxbury they heard that they were broken up." But neither Winthrop nor Rev. John Cotton, the first owner of land in Brookline, came here to live. Another great land owner, who made visits to

the town, was Chief Justice Samuel Sewall,
author of the famous Diary. His son lived on
the southeastern corner of Beacon and Harvard
streets ; but *his* diary is little known, although
the chief justice's frank confessions of love-
making might be matched by his son Samuel's
entry : "January 22, 1714–15, went to Boston,
intending to live at my father's untill I could
find better treatment in my own." Joshua
Scottow of Boston, one of the early grantees,
was the author of "Old Men's Tears for their
own Declensions" (1691), and of "A Narrative
of the Planting of the Massachusetts Colony"
(1694).

The Rev. James Allen, first minister of the
town, published in 1722 a sermon with the title :

> *What shall I Render !*
> a Thanksgiving *SERMON*
> Preached at *Brooklin*, ℜob. 8th, 1722.
> From Psalm CXVI, 12.

Writings by the following Brookline ministers
were collected by Dr. Pierce and have been

Your friend
Hannah Adams.

To face p. 93.

deposited by the First Parish church at the Public Library : Rev. James Allen, seven ; Rev. Nathaniel Potter, one ; Rev. John Pierce, twenty-one, and a manuscript volume of sermons. In 1731 the famous lawyer Jeremy Gridley, later of Brookline, started and edited a weekly paper called the Rehearsal. His style was rather affected.

Miss Hannah Adams, one of the most distinguished women of her day in America, has already been mentioned. She was born at Medfield in 1756, the daughter of a store-keeper of considerable education, who could claim kinship with President John Adams. Poverty came upon her unexpectedly, and her efforts to find a support by making pillow lace, braiding straw, or teaching school were not very successful. She had studied Greek and Latin, and was fond of history and theology. The intolerance of religious authors of the day led her to think of writing a "View of Religious Opinions,"

a work treating of various denominations.   It
appeared in 1784, and with other books brought
her a partial support, eked out in her declining
years by an allowance from Rev. J. S. Buckminster, Hon. Josiah Quincy, Stephen Higginson,
and others who admired her ability and were
attracted by her refined, sensitive nature.

Miss Woods records two incidents which Dr.
Pierce was fond of relating.   Miss Adams had
spent the night with a friend.   In the morning
she prepared for breakfast and went to the door.
The knob "refused to pull out or push in, or
lift up or go down.   It never occurred to her
to *turn* it, so she labored at the refractory thing
till, finding it all in vain, she sat down and waited
till a maid-servant finally came and let her out."
At another time, while boarding with Mr.
Perkins in Leverett street, Boston, she paid a
visit, and then called a carriage to take her
home.   She told the driver to take her to Mr.
Leverett's on Perkins street.   He searched until

eleven o'clock that evening for Perkins street, and at last drove back to his employer, who looked in at the window and exclaimed, " Oh, that's Miss Hannah Adams! carry her to Mr. Perkins's on Leverett street." She was so fond of reading at the Athenæum that the librarian once or twice locked her in while he went to dinner, and upon his return found her still at work, all unconscious of his absence. Miss Adams, when she grew feeble, came to board at Mrs. Walley's, on the northwestern corner of School and Washington streets, west of the site of the present Bethany building, where she died November 15, 1832. A portrait by Chester Harding was painted at the request of friends for the Boston Athenæum. Her autobiography was edited and published after her death by the sister of Rev. J. S. Buckminster, Mrs. Eliza B. Lee, of Brookline.

The Buckminsters came from Thomas Buckminster, author of an almanac printed in London in 1599. His grandson Thomas of Muddy River had a grandson Joseph of Framingham, who married Martha, daughter of Lieutenant Sharp of the Sudbury fight. Their son, Colonel Joseph, was a prominent military and civil officer, and Joseph's son, Colonel William Buckminster, was wounded at Bunker Hill. William's cousin, Rev. Joseph Buckminster, was the father of the pastor of the Brattle street church, and of Eliza who married Thomas Lee. In the Lee house near the Roxbury line and Perkins street, Mrs. Lee wrote some of her best books. Her "Sketches of New England" appeared in 1837, her "Naomi," with its beautiful descriptions of colonial Brookline, in 1848, and her Memoirs of her father and brother in 1849. Thomas Carlyle said that this last work gave him "a much better account of the higher sort of character of New England than anything he had seen since Franklin's writings." She died in Brookline June 22, 1864.

Colonel Thomas Wentworth Higginson, author of "Army Life in a Black Regiment," "Out-Door Papers," "Life of Margaret Fuller," "Common-sense about Women," and "Malbone," spent the greater part of the years 1842 and 1843 in Brookline, as a private tutor to the three young sons of his cousin, Stephen H. Perkins, nephew of Colonel Thomas H. Perkins, the leading merchant of Boston. Here "cousins and friends came, time-honored acquaintances of the old gentleman, eminent public men, Mr. Prescott the historian, or Daniel Webster himself, received like a king." Meanwhile he read Mrs. Lee's "Jean Paul Richter," and Richter's "Siebenkäs," which gave attractive pictures of a life devoted to literature. In the *Atlantic* for January, 1897, he writes : —

"With all this social and intellectual occupation, much of my Brookline life was lonely and meditative; my German romance made me a dreamer, and I spent much time in the woods, nominally botanizing, but in reality trying to adjust myself, being still only nineteen or twenty, to the problems of life." He wandered about the shores of Hammond's pond, where the *Andromeda polifolia* and the pink *Cypripedium* or lady's slipper grew; and climbed the hills while "the sweet bell of the Newton Theological Seminary on its isolated hill would peal out what seemed like the Angelus." In September, 1843, Mr. Higginson returned to Cambridge to study.

In 1871-'72 Miss Harriet F. Woods, a teacher in the schools, published in the Brookline Transcript a series of articles on local history. These sketches were gathered into a volume in 1874 under the title "Historical Sketches of Brookline, Mass." Through the efforts of Miss Abby L. Pierce (Dr. Pierce's daughter), and Mr. Robert S. Davis the financial difficulties were overcome. Miss Woods's work was the result of laborious research and a fondness for her task which opened every door to her. There are few town histories as readable as this anecdotal visitation which Miss Woods made twenty-five years ago, and her memory should always be held in honor for her unselfish efforts to preserve the romance of early Brookline. She was born January 23, 1828, and began her career as a teacher at the age of fifteen. She taught in the public schools of Brookline for twenty-three years. Her death occurred in Newton, where she had gone for her health, October 8, 1879.

Eliakim Littell, founder of *Littell's Living Age*, was born in Burlington, N. J., in 1797, and died in Brookline May 17, 1870. His first paper was the *National Recorder*, which he carried on under this and other names for over twenty years. In 1844 he came to Boston and started the *Living Age*, in which he continued the traditions of the earlier publication. It was later edited by Miss Susan Littell, his daughter. He was the author of the "Compromise Tariff" passed during President Jackson's administration, and took an active interest in Brookline affairs, particularly in those relating to parks and schools.

Hon. Robert C. Winthrop, speaker of the national house of representatives, was a voluminous writer. His orations at Brookline, at Plymouth, at Bunker Hill, at Washington, and at Yorktown, will always be prized. His life of John Winthrop and his own autobiographical sketches are the scholarly work of his leisure hours. He died in Boston November 16, 1894.

George Makepeace Towle lived for a number of years in Brookline, and was a trustee of the Public Library from 1873 to 1887. Many pages of the records are in his handwriting. Mr. Towle was United States consul at Nantes, and later at Bradford. He returned to Boston in 1870 and led an active life as editor and author. He was president of the Papyrus Club in 1880,

MISS HARRIET F. WOODS,

Author of " Historical Sketches of Brookline."

From a photograph lent by W. Y. Cross, Esq. To face p. 101.

a delegate to the Republican national convention at Chicago in 1888, and a state senator in 1890 and 1891. Among his books are "American Society," 1870, "The Eastern Question," 1877, "Principalities of the Danube," 1877, and "Young Folks' Heroes of History," a series of biographies. Mr. Towle died in Brookline August 8, 1893.

Hon. Charles Carleton Coffin, author of "The Boys of '76," "Old Times in the Colonies," "The Story of Liberty," and other stirring books for boys, had but just moved to Shailer street, and had shown, by his fine address before the High School, an interest in the town, when he died, March 2, 1896.

Among the residents of the town who have died or moved away were Frederic Henry Hedge, one of the profound scholars of the middle of the century ; Rev. J. Lewis Dinan, an historical writer of unusual power; Hon. David Hall Rice, author of an able work on " Protective

Philosophy;" William Ware, author of "Zenobia" and " Probus;" Samuel A. Goddard, writer of local history; George B. Emerson, the educator; Commander Winfield S. Schley; Rev. John Seely Stone; Rev. Francis Wharton, a distinguished legal writer; Rev. William Wilberforce Newton; Bishop William Lawrence; Colonel William L. Chase; and Miss Susan E. Blow, writer for the kindergarten.

Of the present writers, who have published books or pamphlets, mention should be made of Edward Atkinson, the economist; Colonel Theodore A. Dodge, the military writer; Percival Lowell, traveler and astronomer; Edward Stanwood, author of a work on " Presidential elections;" J. Elliot Cabot, author of a life of Emerson; Charles Sprague Sargent, author of " The Silva of North America;" Desmond Fitz-Gerald, writer on engineering and water supply; Captain R. G. F. Candage, Bradford Kingman, William I. Bowditch, S. N. D. North, James

Jeffrey Roche, Rev. Reuen Thomas, Samuel T. Dutton, Alfred D. Chandler, Robert Amory, Walter Channing, H. Lincoln Chase, Prentiss Cummings, Hon. M. P. Kennard, J. Geddes, Jr., Reginald H. Howe, Jr., E. P. Vining, S. Arthur Bent, Harrison Ellery, George H. Monroe, Horace W. Fuller, Prescott F. Hall, Dana Estes, Richard Soule, Charles C. Soule, Rev. George C. Lorimer, William D. Orcutt, Prof. John D. Runkle, Rev. Julius H. Ward, Ernest F. Henderson, Henry V. Poor, F. L. Olmsted, Osborne Howes, Andrew J. George, C. A. W. Spencer, Colonel Thomas H. Talbot, Miss Agnes Blake Poor ("Dorothy Prescott"), Miss Eliza Orne White, Mrs. Alicia Aspinwall, Mrs. Blakeslee ("Mary Blake"), Mrs. Mabel Fuller Blodgett, Miss Susan Littell, and some others.

In 1855 and 1856 a boys' newspaper was issued by F. O. Wellman and W. G. Wilson, which was carried on by the latter in 1857 and 1858. The Sagamore, a high school monthly, was started

in 1895. Number one of the Brookline Transcript, a weekly, appeared October 15, 1870, and
was edited by Bradford Kingman until it
suspended in May, 1873. The Brookline Chron-
icle, another weekly newspaper, first appeared
April 9, 1874, edited and published by W. H.
Hutchinson at "the second door east of the
railroad" on Washington street. It later passed
through the hands of Wing & Arthur, C. M.
Vincent, Arthur & Spencer, and finally to Mr.
C. A. W. Spencer (in 1881), who continues the
paper, with Mr. Sidney W. Dean as associate
editor. The Brookline News, an illustrated
weekly, appeared August 7, 1886, edited by Louis
Cassier, and continued its career until March
24, 1888.

Art has been represented in Brookline by
Samuel Colman, the landscape painter, who was
the founder and first president of the American
Society of Painters in Water Color. Mr. Colman
attended the high school in its early days, and

HOME OF ELIAKIM LITTELL, ALTON PLACE.

Founder of " Littell's Living Age."

lived on Walnut street. A miniature and genre painter of note, Richard M. Staigg, lived for some years on Monmouth place. Mr. Dwight Blaney of Walnut street exhibits at the Boston Art club and elsewhere. Mrs. Theo Ruggles Kitson, the sculptor, is the daughter of the late Cyrus W. Ruggles, for many years the village postmaster.

Among the famous artists whose works are owned in the town are : Allston (Theodore Lyman and Charles S. Sargent); Boudin and Monet (Desmond FitzGerald); Cazin (Edward Steese); Copley (Charles S. Sargent); Corot (Mrs. J. L. Gardner, Mrs. C. O. Foster, Wm. E. Cox); Courbet (Isaac R. Thomas); Couture (E. D. Jordan); Rubens (H. S. Howe); Schreyer (W. E. Cox); Stuart (W. I. Bowditch, Mrs. H. L. Eustis, H. M. Cutts, C. P. Gardiner); Sully (Andrew Robeson); Daubigny (Barthold Schlesinger, C. H. W. Foster); Dewing (Edward Stanwood); Diaz (Mrs. J. R. Coolidge, Mrs. A. W. Blake, Joseph H. White); George

Fuller and Inness (Joseph H. White); Lawrence
(E. D. Jordan); Mauve (B. Schlesinger, W. C.
Cotton); Millet (Mrs. A. W. Blake); Reynolds (E.
D. Jordan, H. S. Howe); Vinton (High School);
Bonheur and Etty (Mrs. D. D. Addison).

In the arts Brookline stands preëminent.
Frederick Law Olmsted, of the firm of F. L.
and J. C. Olmsted, has long been the most
distinguished landscape architect in the United
States.   From the firm, which at one time
included the late Charles Eliot, son of President
Eliot of Harvard, many young men have received
their early professional training.   The death of
two of these, Henry Sargent Codman and his
brother Philip Codman, sons of Mr. James M.
Codman, deprived the younger school of landscape architects of two of its promising members.
As early as 1850, Mr. Olmsted became interested
in landscape gardening and spent a summer in
England.   Before the breaking out of the civil
war he traveled in the South, studying the social

and agricultural conditions of the people. His observations in each case were published, and at the outbreak of the war "The Cotton Kingdom," a condensation of his writings, was issued in London and was frequently quoted.

During the war he was actively engaged in the improvement of the sanitary condition of the Union forces. Since then he has been the leading expert in laying out the larger parks and park-systems, as Morningside and Riverside parks, New York; Prospect and Washington parks, Brooklyn; Washington and Jackson parks, Chicago, with their parkways, and the parkways of Boston. He was the landscape architect of Central park, New York, and the first commissioner of the National park of the Yosemite.

In architecture as in landscape gardening Brookline has for many years been the home of a leader. Henry Hobson Richardson's work has left its impress on a large share of the public buildings erected in America in recent years.

His best work began with the Brattle street church, Boston, in 1871. Soon after he was chosen architect of Trinity church, Boston, and gave much of his time and thought to the beautiful building which was finished in 1877. The Albany city hall, the public libraries at Woburn, Malden, Quincy and Burlington, Sever hall and Austin hall (the law school) at Harvard, the railroad stations of the Boston & Albany, the board of trade at Cincinnati, and the court-house in Pittsburg — these and many others show his power through the use of mass and form rather than detail. And many libraries throughout New England, not of his hand, show the influence of his free treatment of the Romanesque. He was a great-grandson of Dr. Joseph Priestley, the discoverer of oxygen, and showed a brilliancy and magnetism worthy of his inheritance. Mr. Richardson died in Brookline, April 28, 1886. His wife is descended from Ebenezer Craft, who built the Craft house on Huntington avenue in 1709.

THE HOME OF DR. S. A. SHURTLEFF, BOYLSTON STREET.

William Ware wrote "Zenobia" in the room at the extreme left.

From a photograph lent by Dr. Augustine Shurtleff.

To face p. 109.

Another architect of national reputation is Henry Ives Cobb of Chicago, who was born in Brookline, August 19, 1859. He designed the fisheries building for the World's Fair at Chicago, in 1893, one of the best in that group of harmonious buildings which gave the "White City" its fame. He is the architect of the University of Chicago and of the post office building in Chicago, now (1897) being constructed. Among the present residents of the town are a number of the leading architects of the United States.

On every telephone instrument of the Bell Telephone Company are the words, "Blake transmitter." Francis Blake, nephew of the late Commodore George S. Blake of Brookline, was born in Needham, but went from the Brookline high school to the United States coast survey, where he received scientific training. While engaged in this work he took up experimental physics as a pastime. In 1878 the Blake transmitter was devised, and was adopted at once by the Bell Telephone Company as far superior to any transmitter then in use. Mr. Blake lives at Weston, but keeps his interest in the town, and attended recently a meeting of the High School Alumni Association.

In 1868 E. S. Ritchie & Sons, manufacturers of philosophical instruments, moved from Boston to Brookline, and established themselves at the corner of Harvard and Washington streets. For many years the firm has made marine compasses for the United States navy. Those in use on the monitors during the rebellion were liquid compasses designed and made in Brookline. In their present quarters on Cypress street, southeast of the Boston & Albany circuit, the firm make fine apparatus for high schools and colleges.

Near by is the factory of Mr. John Shields, where fishing tackle is made in large quantities. On Station street the Holtzer-Cabot Electric Company is engaged in the manufacture of electrical appliances.

THE SCHOOLS.

Education in Brookline has been a continuous factor in the town's development since March 8, 1685, when the inhabitants of Muddy River petitioned "for a writinge school for theire children." The next year Boston freed the hamlet from town rates with the understanding that Muddy River would provide an able reading and writing master. The first school-house seems to have stood a little south of the southwest corner of Harvard and School streets, facing School lane. A brook, which now runs below ground, flowed through the low land a little west of the lane and behind the school-house; crossing the Cambridge road it watered a large tree on the northeastern corner, and in its course touched the meadows sloping eastward from the old Aspinwall house.

The second school was built on the eastern side of the lane. There was a large wood-pile outside, and the half-seasoned and weather-soaked logs were cut into firewood by some of the boys, while others brought from Squire Sharp's house up the road a few live coals in an iron skillet. In time a second story was added, and here Miss Catherine Stearns, with the occasional aid of older pupils or of another teacher, carried on the school for many years. In 1855 the building was sold and moved to Washington street, where it remained until it was pulled down in May, 1896.

The first school-house built by Brookline as a town is said to have stood in the triangle at the junction of Walnut and Warren streets. Permission to build was given in 1713. In 1728, and for fifty years after, there were contentions regarding the number of schools to be kept. At the November meeting in the latter year two were ordered, "one to stand in the new lane

[Cypress street] between Mr. Allin's and Water-town Road [Washington street], beyond the bridge [over Village brook] as near the bridge as there can be a spot of land for it." If this vote was carried out, a school-house must once have stood on or near the present High School playground.

In 1793 a brick school-house was built at the corner of Walnut and Warren streets where school was kept from April till November. Here also Dr. Pierce held his Wednesday after-noon catechisms for many years.

Of Isaac Adams who taught here for twenty years, many strange tales survive. His methods of punishment are contrasted with his devotion to his young wife and his half-frantic grief long after her death. He spanked the unruly boy with a leather strap, or made him stand before the class with his nose wedged into the split end of a sapling. In times of great disorder he would pile the boys in a pyramid on the floor and spank the unlucky one at the top.   For the girls he had a unipod or one-legged stool, on which a wrong-doer must balance herself for an hour or more.

The brick school was used also for town meetings.   The services and the address by Dr. Pierce in honor of Washington at his death were held at the church on the present parsonage grounds, but the procession formed at the school-house and marched thither.

The present Pierce hall, next to the First Parish church, was dedicated as a school January 1, 1825.   The town hall, on the second floor, was used also for singing-classes and lectures.

The lyceum movement gained such force in Brookline from 1832, through the enthusiasm of Mr. Isaac Thayer, Dr. S. A. Shurtleff, and others, that the " Lyceum of the Town of Brookline " was incorporated in 1841.   Lyceum hall, which still stands west of the site of the Punch Bowl tavern, opposite the end of Walnut street, was soon erected. The lectures and courses of study did much for education in the town. Music, phrenology, science and literature in turn became the talk of the day. The young girls delighted in Mr. Christopher Duncan, "feasting one's eyes on his beauty," and in Mr. Charles Emerson, "a delightful specimen of his creator's workmanship." R. W. Emerson, Hillard, Rufus Choate, and Dr. Webster, subsequently the murderer of Parkman, went through the ordeal of feminine criticism.

The town on March 6, 1843, voted to establish a high school; Dr. Pierce, Rev. William H. Shailer, and Samuel Philbrick, Esq., the school committee for that year, were untiring advocates of public education. The present Pierce hall was chosen for this purpose, and Mr. B. H. Rhoades became the first principal. He and his successor, Mr. Hezekiah Shailer, brother of Mr. Shailer, the Baptist minister, were graduates

of Boston University.   Mr. Shailer served from
May 4, 1846, to April 26, 1852.   The principals
since that time have been : —

George Moore, May, 1852, to July, 1852.

William P. Atkinson, a graduate of Harvard,
September, 1852, to February 28, 1853.

Rev. John N. Bellows, February 28, 1853, to
May, 1853.

Isaac Coffin, a graduate of Dartmouth, April
26, 1853, to April, 1854.

J. Emory Hoar, (Harvard,) April 10, 1854, to
July, 1888.

Frederic T. Farnsworth, (Tufts,) September,
1888, to June 26, 1891.

Daniel S. Sanford, a graduate of Yale,
September 7, 1891 —.

In Mr. Rhoades's day there were two weeks of
vacation preceding the first Monday in May,
three weeks preceding the first Monday in
September, and Thanksgiving week; also Fourth
of July and Christmas.   Among the students

BROOKLINE HIGH SCHOOL, GORHAM AVENUE.

To face p. 117.

during the first year were Samuel Colman, founder and first president of the American society of painters in water-colors; and Edward S. Philbrick, treasurer of the Massachusetts anti-slavery society and a distinguished civil engineer. Two of the students later married well-known citizens, Dr. Tappan E. Francis and Captain R. G. F. Candage.

During the rule of Mr. Bellows some boy each Saturday chose for his declamation, "The Village Blacksmith." When he reached the words "They love to see the flaming forge and hear the bellows roar," a titter went round the room. After a time the principal lost his patience.

In 1857 the high school at the southeastern corner of School and Prospect streets was completed, and served until the present building was finished in 1895.

The first appropriation for the new high school building which stands at the corner of

Tappan street and Gorham avenue, facing the Common, was made January 25, 1895. The dedication took place November 19, 1895. The severe external appearance is due to a desire to keep the cost of the building within the $200,000 appropriated, but the interior, with its heating and ventilating apparatus, its assembly hall, its special accommodations for science teaching, art study, and physical training, fulfills its purpose admirably. The grounds were laid out by Olmsted, Olmsted & Eliot. The cost of furnishing was about $25,000, making a total cost of $225,000. There are 19,750 square feet in the ground area.

April 22, 1872, Mr. William T. Reid was appointed superintendent of schools, the first person to hold this office, and resigned in 1875. Mr. Reid was perhaps too fond of frequent examinations to please all people. He is now said to be very successful as master of a private school in California.

In 1879 Mr. D. H. Daniels was made superintendent of grammar and primary schools. The master of the high school was responsible to the school committee alone. At the time of Mr. Daniels's resignation in 1890, after a term of service longer than that of any teacher who had served the town, Mr. Samuel T. Dutton of New Haven was appointed superintendent of schools. The feeling that the harmonious working of all the schools in the town would be best subserved by having one responsible head, has been amply justified by the unity of purpose and spirit of coöperation manifested since Mr. Dutton's appointment. A wider application of this principle was made in establishing the Brookline Education Society on March 13, 1895. Here parents and teachers meet to discuss the problems of public education and the home care of children.

Mr. Hoar, the master of the high school, had resigned in 1888, after serving the town for thirty-four years. A large number of the older citizens of Brookline received their education under him; in remembrance of this early training and association, Mr. Hoar's pupils asked him to sit to F. P. Vinton for an oil portrait which they gave in 1896 to the new high school, where it now hangs.

His successor, Mr. F. T. Farnsworth, resigned his position in 1891, and Mr. Daniel S. Sanford of Stamford, Connecticut, was appointed. Largely through the efforts of Mr. Dutton and Mr. Sanford, the various educational influences of the town have been brought into sympathy.

The following statistics are for 1896–97 : —

Number of children in town between five and fifteen years of age . . .	2,529
Value of school property	$910,455 00
Assessed valuation in Brookline . . .	$60,996,800 00
Total expenditures for schools	119,521 79
Percentage for schools	0019
Cost of instruction for each pupil . . .	39 20
Whole number of pupils	3,168
Total number of teachers in day schools	109
School buildings	16

THE EDWARD DEVOTION SCHOOL, HARVARD STREET.

From a photograph lent by Mrs. A. J. Waite.

To face p. 121.

THE CLASSICAL SCHOOL.

About the year 1822 Richard Sullivan, General Dearborn, Ebenezer Francis, Lewis Tappan, Rev. John Pierce, Oliver Whyte, Elijah Corey, Timothy Corey, and others, formed a corporation for the purpose of establishing a classical school in Brookline. They purchased land on the northern side of Boylston street east of Cypress street, and erected a fine school building. Later the northerly addition was built for boarding the students. In 1830 Mr. GideonThayer, founder of Chauncy Hall School, bought the place as a branch of his Boston school, where delicate boys could have better air. Mr. Thayer was a kindly Christian gentleman, whose connection with the town was the means of many improvements. George B. Emerson, LL. D., the eminent schoolmaster and naturalist, was the next owner of the property; and during this period William Ware wrote, in the north parlor of the house, his historical romance called "Zenobia, or the Fall of Palmyra." About 1838 Dr. S. A. Shurtleff, a prominent physician of Boston, purchased the place, and continued its scholarly associations. At Dr. Shurtleff's death in 1873, his son Dr. Augustine Shurtleff came into possession of the house and made it his home until 1881.

LIBRARIES.

The first library in Brookline was started in 1825 through the efforts of Rev. John Pierce, who became president, Deacon Otis Withington, who served as secretary, Deacon John Robinson, treasurer, and the town clerk, Oliver Whyte, who became librarian. The rules were adopted December 27, 1825. At the bottom of the book label were the words : —

"The library is kept in the house of the librarian."

Mr. Whyte lived on what is now the south-eastern corner of Walnut and High streets, or between Walnut street and Village lane (*i. e.* Elm place). The subscription was five dollars a year for the first and second years, and two dollars thereafter. The library was kept later at the shoe shop of John Leeds on Washington street, a little east of the Public Library, near Chase's express office.

At my request Mr. Baker has described a movement which did much to prepare the way for the modern public library. He says : —

"In the autumn of 1846, a number of young men, mechanics and others, in this town, having a desire for some opportunity whereby they could improve themselves and obtain a larger range of information and mental improvement, as well as a better knowledge of books and of what was being done in different parts of the country, agreed to hire some place where they could meet evenings and dull days when they were obliged to be idle. Each one was to contribute whatever he might have of books, or papers, whether of biography, travel, fiction, or other works that might be of interest. In pursuance of that object a small room was hired and fitted up with some rough shelves and tables; each one brought his contribution of books or other matter, and they were used interchangeably. They also subscribed for and

BROOKLINE PUBLIC LIBRARY, WASHINGTON STREET.

took newspapers from Boston, New York, Baltimore, Philadelphia, Washington and New Orleans.

"This room was first opened in the autumn, and was kept open in the evening through the winter and summer, so that the members could visit it when they had an opportunity (each member having a key). They also occasionally hired a larger room and had discussions on the topics of the day, or read papers on some subject, or recited or read poetry or prose.

"This room was used until the fall of 1849, when the news of the finding of gold in California reached the town. Several of the members were taken with the gold fever, and various circumstances arising to call others away, the association was disbanded.

"I cannot recall the names of all who belonged, but among them were: Isaac R. Atwood, J. D. Long, Elisha Hall, Jr., Edward

Hall, Eben Haskell, Isaac Farrington, Jr., Abraham C. Small, B. F. Baker, and Oliver Cousens."

One of the originators, Elisha Hall, asked Horace Mann to draft a bill authorizing towns and cities to raise and appropriate money to establish and maintain public libraries. The bill became a law in 1851.

The public library of Brookline was one of the first in Massachusetts instituted under the general statute of 1851. It was established by vote of the town, March 30, 1857, and opened to the public on Wednesday, December 2, 1857, at 2 P. M., with 900 volumes on the shelves. The first home of the public library was "the hall on the first floor of the town hall," now the police station, which was afterward moved to the west side of Prospect street, to make room for the present Town Hall. Brookline was at that time the richest town of its size in the state, and the first appropriations were as large as the law allowed: $934 for its foundation—being $1.00 for each of the ratable polls of the preceding year—and $233 for current expenses. The sum of $300 was appropriated for fitting up the hall. Mr. J. Emory Hoar was chosen librarian, November 11, 1857, and held the office until other duties compelled him to relinquish the cares of the library, September 19, 1871. Miss Mary A. Bean was at the same meeting elected to the position, which she held until her death, September 4, 1893. November 21, 1893, the trustees elected Mr. Charles K. Bolton of the Harvard college library to fill the vacancy. He took charge January 2, 1894. The first assistant, Miss Amelia A. Woods, died February 5, 1896, having been connected with the library for twenty-seven years.

The present hall, reference room, and fiction alcoves comprise the building which was erected in 1869, and opened for the delivery of books on October 18th. In 1888 the north wing was added, to relieve the cramped condition of the book-shelves, and in 1892 Gardner Hall, the new reading room, was opened to the public.

Benefactions of importance should be noted : a gift of $10,000 in 1871 from John L. Gardner, Esq., a bequest of $5,000 from Martin L. Hall in his will of the same year, and gifts from John S. Wright, J. M. Howe, Mrs. Samuel Philbrick, Abijah W. Goddard, Mrs. D. W. Russell, and Frank A. Russell. The last gift was to aid the music collection, which was opened to the public in August, 1895.

In answer to the first request of the trustees for donations, the librarian reported February 1, 1858,— two months after the library was opened, — gifts from the following people: William I. Bowditch, James A. Dupee, Jeremiah Hill, Thomas Parsons, Wm. H. Jameson, Theodore Lyman, Society of the New Jerusalem, Daniel H. Rogers, J. S. Warren, Waldo Maynard, Robert S. Davis, Miss Lucy Searle, T. P.

Chandler, William K. Melcher, F. J. Williams, William Nichols, Jr., Miss Elizabeth Pierce, Charles D. Head, Mrs. Ingersoll, F. W. Prescott, John Howe, J. W. Thornton, William A. Wellman, F. O. Wellman, William B. Towne, William H. Towne, J. H. Putnam, B. B. Davis, Alfred Winsor, George G. Stoddard, Hon. Henry Wilson, C. S. F. Binney, J. B. Taylor, William Lincoln, Charles C. Soule, T. E. Francis, Edward Wilder, J. H. Wellman, Miss Annie L. Brackett, and Miss M. H. Snow. The works donated numbered 1052.

The following table shows the increase in number of volumes and in circulation, with the appropriations in the years named : —

Year.	Volumes in Library.	Circulation for Home Use.	Appropriation.
1858 . . .	2,137	(two months) 3,600	$240.00
1868 . . .	10,500	18,144	1,000.00
1878 . . .	20,332	50,427	4,000.00
1888 . . .	32,700	43,464	7,000.00
1896 . . .	43,768	88,633	12,000.00

UNITARIAN.

First Parish.

For over a century the First Parish church was "the Church of Christ in Brookline".—the town's church. As such its history was a part of the history of the town. (See page 19.)

Toward the end of Dr. Pierce's life, the Congregational church became divided into two parties. The pastor of the First church allied himself with neither, preferring to remain true to the old traditions which associated the church with the whole town. At his death in 1849, his colleague, Rev. Frederic Newman Knapp, took up the parish duties as his successor. As the meeting-house was often cold, without a cellar or furnace, a new building was erected in 1848. Dr. Pierce was carried to the church on December 1st, and assisted at the dedication. Once more he was taken to the church in a chair on August 18th to hear the new organ, for he had always been fond of music. His favorite tune " Old Hundred " was sung at his request. He remained seated because, as he said playfully, he " no longer belonged to the rising genera-tion." He was borne home by loving hands, and as he grew weaker, friends from all the neighboring towns came to bring him flowers and fruit, wishing to brighten his last hours. Mr. Shailer, the Baptist minister, whom he called his " oldest son," visited him three times each week during the summer, and shaved him, or passed the time in reading aloud or in conversation. He died in the forenoon of August 24, 1849. At his funeral the baptismal font was filled with white flowers, and the coffin bore a wreath placed there by one of the children of the Sunday school. The services were conducted by Mr. Shailer, Dr. Lowell and Mr. Knapp. Dr. Pierce was not remarkable as a preacher, but his

life was a beautiful example of entire devotion
to a town, a people, and to the minister's
calling.

In 1856 Rev. Frederic Henry Hedge became
pastor of the church and remained until 1872,
although part of his time after the first year was
occupied in Cambridge as a professor at the
Divinity school. Dr. Hedge married Dr. Pierce's
daughter. His scholarship and eloquence were
worthy companions of his character.

In 1873 Rev. Howard N. Brown was called
to succeed him. During his ministry a beautiful
church was erected on the site of the second and
third meeting houses built in 1805 and 1848. It
was dedicated April 19, 1893. Mr. Brown
upheld the traditions of his predecessors by
taking an active interest in the schools and
in the public library. The trustees of the
library in their report for 1896, said: " As
chairman of the library committee for several
years, he brought a scholarly intelligence and

REVEREND JOHN PIERCE, D. D.

Minister of the town, 1797-1849.

devotion to his administration of affairs, which are well worthy of emulation."

Rev. William H. Lyon became pastor of the First Parish, May 8, 1896.

The old custom of ringing the bell at seven o'clock every morning, at noon, and at nine o'clock every evening has been continued through all these years of change. And still upon the town records will be found an annual appropriation for this purpose.

BAPTIST.

At Dr. Pierce's ordination there were two baptists in the town, members of the First Baptist church in Newton. As early as 1805 a new interest was awakened, and in 1810 about twenty young people, as a result of a special religious impression, joined the church in Newton. After holding meetings at private houses for some months in 1827, a growing need was manifested for better accommodations. In March, 1828, a building twenty-six feet by

thirty-six feet was erected on the corner of
Harvard and Washington streets. On the 5th
of June the Baptist Church in Brookline was
publicly recognized, with thirty-six members.
In October Elijah Corey, Timothy Corey and
Thomas Griggs were chosen deacons. The
same year the first building seemed to be too
small; on the 20th of November the second
building, which stood west of the first, was
dedicated. The three deacons, together with
David Coolidge and Elijah Corey, Jr., agreed
to bear the expense. In March, 1830, the
Rev. Joseph Driver became their pastor.
April 14, 1831, Rev. Joseph A. Warne began his
ministry, which continued until December 31,
1836. In Mr. Warne's time baptism was
administered in the salt waters of Muddy river
near the present bridge at the end of Washington street, while Mr. Shailer preferred to go to
the Charles. Mr. Warne "did much to beget
and mature a love for sound doctrine."

September 1, 1837, Rev. William H. Shailer having accepted an invitation, became pastor of the church. During his ministry, which ended January 31, 1854, his devotion to the welfare of the church and town were untiring. He was the moving spirit in establishing the first high school, and Shailer hall, in the new high school, is a witness to his love for education.

Rev. Nehemiah M. Perkins was pastor from May 20, 1855, to August, 1858, when failing health compelled him to relinquish work.

The new church building at the corner of Harvard and Pierce streets was dedicated December 1, 1858.

Rev. William Lamson, D. D., accepted a call and began his ministry December 1, 1859. He was an eloquent and earnest preacher, and was greatly beloved. The church grew to a membership of 237 before he resigned in February, 1875. A memorial volume was published by his wife.

Rev. Henry C. Mabie, the pastor from January 1, 1876, to August 1, 1879, was followed by **Rev. J. B. Brackett, D. D.**, pastor from May 1, 1880, until May 1, 1888.   Rev. O. P. Gifford served as pastor from January 1, 1890, to November 30, 1891, and his able ministry is still remembered. He was followed by Rev. Nathan E. Wood, D.D., who was pastor of the church from March 1, 1892, until August 26, 1894.   Rev. Edward Braislin, his successor, announced his acceptance of a call January 6, 1895, but resigned in July, owing to poor health, having officiated but two Sundays.   He was followed by the Rev. Thomas S. Barbour, who began his pastorate September 20, 1896.

Many of the older families have been associated for generations with the church, including those of Griggs, Corey, Davis and Stearns, and many of the present generation of members, at least, have been active in the town government, including Benjamin F. Baker, H. Lincoln Chase,

STONEHURST, BEACON STREET.

The home of Eben D. Jordan, Esq.

Captain Rufus G. F. Candage, Emery B. Gibbs, and George Brooks. Rev. Barnas Sears, at one time president of Brown University, was a member of the church. Thomas Simmons, Helen M. Griggs, Sarah Davis, Elizabeth Morse, and Martha A. Sanderson, all members of the church, spent their lives in missionary fields.

CONGREGATIONAL.

Harvard Church.

The Harvard Congregational Society was organized August 26, 1844, but the church has always been, and in its original constitution was, simply and designedly called " The Harvard Church." The first place of worship was the present Bethany building on the western corner of School and Washington streets. Here during the pastorate of Rev. Richard Salter Storrs, Jr., the first minister, installed October 22, 1845, there gathered each Sunday a congregation of seventy-five to one hundred people. Although the young Andover student had been enjoined to make this his permanent home, according to the good old custom of his father's day, his remarkable ability seemed to call him to a larger field. In a year (October 27, 1846,) he was dismissed to Brooklyn, New York, where, as pastor of the Church of the Pilgrims, his fiftieth anniversary of service was recently celebrated as an event of national interest.

Rev. Joseph Haven, Jr., became pastor December 31, 1846, but resigned December 12, 1850, to become a professor at Amherst College, and later at the Theological Seminary of Chicago. Six months later, on June 5, 1851, Rev. Matson Meier Smith was installed as pastor of the Harvard church, where he remained until November 23, 1858, when his views began to undergo a change which led him, after a pastorate at Bridgeport, into the Episcopal communion. His successor, Rev. J. Lewis Diman of Fall River, began his work March 15, 1860, and served until June 29, 1864, when he became professor of history and political economy in Brown University. He had studied under such German scholars as Erdmann, Tholock, and Baron Bunsen, and was by education as well as by temperament, better fitted for a professorship than a pastorate. If he seemed to lack adaptability, it was chiefly owing to the fact that his was a singularly sensitive, æsthetic nature, trained by association with the most learned men of his time.

Dr. Thomas, in his historical address delivered in 1894, says: "That a church in its infancy and early youth should have been able to command the services of such men as these I have named, is among the remarkable facts in its history."

Mr. Diman was followed by Rev. C. C. Carpenter, June 29, 1865, to September 18, 1867, and by Rev. C. Maurice Wines, November 12, 1868, to April 27, 1870. From this time to the installation of Rev. Reuen Thomas, May 4, 1875, the church had no regular pastor.

In May, 1873, a new church was completed at the corner of Harvard and Marion streets. This beautiful Gothic building, designed by E. Tuckerman Potter, has cost, with the land, about $230,000. Martin L. Hall was one of those who gave most largely to prevent the church from having any debt; which has been among its traditions from the beginning.

In the historical address mentioned above, Dr. Thomas alludes to his coming to Brookline from his large parish in London, and says: "I loved 'the common people,' as they are called. I was a people's man." And a little farther on he adds: "I desire to welcome and use the resources of all true and high scholarship. I love communion with the poets, the philosophers and the scientists, believing them to be subsidiary but indispensable aids in getting at the intellect and heart of life."

Leyden Church.

In 1896 a movement was started for a new Congregational church near the Beaconsfield terraces. The Leyden church was organized October 4th, and on November 4th the Rev. Harris G. Hale of Warren, Mass., was installed as pastor. Services are now (1897) held in the Beaconsfield casino; but a movement has already been started to purchase land and build a chapel. The organization has been unusually effective and successful.

EPISCOPAL.

Saint Paul's.

On Sunday, July 8, 1849, Dr. Clark, bishop of Rhode Island, conducted a service in the Town Hall. This was the beginning of the Episcopal church in Brookline. In October Rev. William Horton was elected rector, and continued the services at the Town Hall. In 1850 Augustus Aspinwall offered a site for a church at the corner of the present St. Paul street and

Aspinwall avenue, then called Perry's lane, a part of the old family estate. Richard Upjohn was selected to make the plans, and long years after he felt that the present structure was one of his greatest achievements. Mr. Horton resigned in May, and in September Rev. John S. Stone, D. D., was chosen rector. The church was consecrated December 23, 1852. Dr. Stone resigned in October, 1862, and Rev. Francis Wharton, D. D., was elected to fill the vacancy. He resigned in November, 1869, and Rev. William Wilberforce Newton, D. D., was elected. Dr. Newton resigned in March, 1875, and Rev. Leonard Kip Storrs, D. D., was elected in the following December, and is the present rector. Dr. Storrs is also a trustee of the Public Library.

The chapel on the north side of the church was added during Dr. Stone's term of service; and the rectory was built in memory of Mr. Henry S. Chase by his children, after his death in 1885. The parish house, constructed from designs by Mr. J. A. Schweinfurth, was completed in 1896, and is in perfect architectural harmony with the church.

There are memorial tablets in the church to Henry Savage Chase, Harrison Fay, Rev. Dr. Stone and James S. Amory. A part of the inscription on the tablet dedicated to the memory of Dr. Stone reads as follows : " Rev. John Seeley Stone, D. D., Rector of this Parish, 1852–1862. Powerful as a preacher, beloved as a pastor, he was remarkable for the length and character of his services to the American Episcopal church in which he was born and nurtured."

The memorial windows in the church bear the names of William Chadbourne; Mary Lilley Campbell, wife of W. F. Humphrey; Marland Cogswell Hobbs; Lila G. Floyd and Edward E. Floyd, Jun.; Colonel William Latham Candler ; Sarah Leverett Chase; Thomas Parsons; and Hon. William Aspinwall, who died in 1823.

All Saints.

All Saints church was organized November 1, 1894, the first service having been held on September 30th. Rev. Daniel Dulany Addison of Beverly accepted his election as rector November 25th, and was installed at the first morning service in the Beaconsfield casino, December 23d. Early in the new year — February 8, 1895 — the parish was incorporated. In September, 1895, the chapel at the south-western corner of Beacon street and Dean road was ready, and since then the parish has had a steady and encouraging growth.

An attractive year book gives information concerning the organization and work of the church. The wardens of All Saints are (1897) William P. Shreve and Frederick P. Addicks.

Church of Our Saviour.

The Church of Our Saviour on Carlton street was organized February 19, 1868, and the beautiful church edifice, built in memory of

Amos Lawrence by his sons, Amos A. Lawrence and William R. Lawrence, was consecrated in March, 1868. The first rector, Rev. Elliott D. Tomkins, was succeeded in 1875 by Rev. Frank L. Norton, D. D. In March, 1877, Rev. Reginald H. Howe, D. D., son of Bishop Howe of Central Pennsylvania, became rector.

At different times the Lawrence family and the parish have made additions, until the church, the parish house, the rectory, the cloister and the choir room form a group of most picturesque buildings in the midst of a rapidly increasing community. The parish house was erected in 1879, the rectory and cloister in 1885, and the memorial transept and choir room in 1893. In the nave of the church there is a remarkable window by Sir Edward Burne-Jones, and in the chancel three good specimens of the Tiffany favrile glass. The parish numbers among its members many of the representative people of that part of Brookline known as Longwood, as well as a number from the Back Bay. In the Roxbury district adjoining, it finds a large field for its charitable work. The sittings in the church are all free.

CATHOLIC.

Our Lady of the Assumption.

In 1852, Rev. Michael O'Beirne was appointed to organize Catholic congregations in Brookline and Brighton. While St. Mary's Church of the Assumption was being built in Andem place, Brookline, mass was celebrated in Lyceum hall. The first services in the new church took place on Christmas day of the year following, although the church was not dedicated until September 24, 1854. Father O'Beirne was already in failing health, and in December, 1854, Rev. J. M. Finotti took charge of the parish. He lived at the end of Harrison place, now extended and called Kent street, and is well remembered as a learned and respected leader in his work. His actual appointment as pastor dated from

December 8, 1856. The church having been injured by fire in 1855, it was enlarged until the seating capacity reached over one thousand. Shortly after Easter, 1872, Rev. P. F. Lamb succeeded Father Finotti. He suffered from poor health and soon found the strain of a large parish had overtaxed his powers. A southern trip did little toward restoring his strength, and he died in July, 1873. The same month Rev. L. J. Morris was appointed pastor of the parish, where, writes Father Butler, "he immediately endeared himself to his new flock and secured their hearty coöperation."

On the 1st of September, 1880, ground was broken for a new church on the western corner of Harvard street and Linden place. The corner stone was laid June 19, 1881, when Rev. C. H. McKenna, O. S. B., delivered the sermon and Archbishop Williams took part in the ceremonies. In October, 1882, services took place for the first time in the new church (in the basement). On the 22d of August, 1886, the dedicatory services were held. The archbishop officiated, and had the assistance of the neighboring clergy. Rt. Rev. P. T. O'Reilly of Springfield preached in the morning, and the St. Cecilia mass was rendered. In the evening Bishop Bradley delivered an eloquent sermon.

The church is 168 feet in length, built of brick, with trimmings of Longmeadow brownstone. The architecture is Gothic, with a tower on the Harvard street side, near the crossing of the nave and transept, rising to a height of 146 feet. Peabody and Stearns were the architects.

Perhaps the best known family connected with the church is that represented by the descendants of the late James Driscoll, who came to Brookline in 1838. His son, Michael Driscoll, is (1897) superintendent of streets and sewers, and a member of the school committee.

Saint Laurence Chapel.

On September 6, 1896, the corner stone was laid for the Saint Laurence chapel on Boylston street, near Chestnut Hill avenue. The dedication took place May 2, 1897.

SWEDENBORGIAN.

The Church of the New Jerusalem in Brookline was organized in April, 1857, and the pretty old English stone church, on the triangular lot bounded by High, Irving and Allerton streets, was built in 1862. High street at that time turned at the church and followed the present Irving street to Walnut street, so that it stood on a fine open eminence surrounded by fields.

The first pastor was Rev. T. B. Hayward, who was followed in 1861 by Rev. John C. Ager. His successors were Rev. S. M. Warren, Rev. Abiel Silver, Rev. Warren Goddard, Jr., who was installed in April, 1874, and Rev. Willard H. Hinkley, who served from September, 1881, to August, 1895. The present pastor, Rev. Julian K. Smyth, was called in the autumn of 1896.

The chairman of the church committee is Hon. Albert Mason, judge of the superior court, and Mr. T. R. Shewell is the clerk.

METHODIST EPISCOPAL.
Saint Mark's.

As early as 1863, Rev. Gilbert Haven of Boston, famous later as an abolitionist and bishop, held services Sunday evenings in the old Town Hall, but a Methodist society was not organized until the spring of 1873. The Congregationalists had just left the Bethany building on Washington street, and this building was purchased and rededicated on June 23, 1873. The Rev. E. D. Winslow was asked to become the pastor. In the spring of 1874, Rev. Mark Trafton succeeded him, and at this time the church was in a prosperous condition. The financial troubles of 1876 bore so hard upon the society that the Bethany building passed into other hands. From 1876 to 1879 Sunday services were held in the Town Hall. In 1879, under the leadership of Rev. William McDonald, a chapel was built on the southeastern corner of Cypress and Washington streets, on land purchased by the society. From that time the Methodist church has prospered. The Rev. John H. Twombly was the last pastor in the chapel, which had become too small and was sold in 1892. The year before this 25,000 feet of land at the corner of Park and Vernon streets were purchased, and on April 9, 1892, the corner stone of St. Mark's was laid with fitting cere- monies. Rev. William N. Brodbeck, the pastor, gave an historical address, and was followed by Bishops Hurst and Foster. For five years services were held in the Town Hall. In April, 1894, Rev. William I. Haven, son of Rev. Gilbert Haven, was appointed pastor ; during his pastor- ate the building has been completed. The

building committee included James Rothwell
(deceased), W. W. Potter, J. E. Rothwell, R. A.
Flanders, A. G. Brewer, L. T. Lyon, and Rev.
W. I. Haven.

The architect of the church is Mr. George A.
Clough of Brookline. The nave is 150 feet in
length, and 75 feet in width. The walls are of
variegated Brighton ledge stone, with trimmings
of gray Nova Scotia sandstone. A beautiful
tower rises at the north-eastern corner of the
nave. The general effect is not unlike that
of the Romanesque cathedral churches of
southern France. Within, a fine sculptured oak
screen divides the nave from the apse at the
transept. The heavy columns of Indiana lime-
stone are especially noticeable. The large rose
window at the north end of the nave is a
memorial to James M. Burgess. In the transept
are memorial windows, the one at the western
end to Mrs. Rachel Moore, and that at the
eastern end to Mr. Trafton, Mr. McDonald and

Mr. Twombly, early pastors of the church. The church has placed a tablet in the vestibule in memory of James Rothwell, first chairman of the building committee. Mr. Haven gave the pulpit in memory of his father, and Mrs. Haven gave the baptismal font.

The tablet in memory of Mr. Rothwell reads :

ERECTED BY
SAINT MARK'S CHURCH
IN GRATEFUL REMEMBRANCE
OF
JAMES ROTHWELL,
WHOSE GENEROSITY MADE POSSIBLE
THIS
HOUSE OF WORSHIP.

St. Mark's was dedicated October 14, 15 and 18, 1896. Bishop Charles H. Fowler preached the dedication sermon. Portraits of Bishop Gilbert Haven, Rev. W. I. Haven, and views of the church may be found in *Zion's Herald* for October 21st.

The pastors of the church have been : E. D. Winslow, 1873 ; Mark Trafton, 1874–75 ; W. S.

Robinson (supplied), 1876 ; Elijah R. Watson (supplied), 1877–78 ; William McDonald, 1879–1881 ; Joshua Gill, 1882 ; William G. Leonard, 1883–84 ; Joshua Gill, 1885–86 ; John H. Twombly, 1887–1890 ; William Nast Brodbeck, 1891–93 ; William Ingraham Haven, 1894 to date (1897).

UNIVERSALIST.

On Sunday, November 29, 1891, Rev. Charles Conklin held a Universalist mission service in Union hall at the corner of High and Walnut streets. January 8, 1892, a temporary organization was effected, and Mr. Conklin, state missionary, became president of the new parish ; in March, the Methodist chapel at the corner of Cypress and Washington streets was hired for Sunday services. August 15, 1892, Rev. T. E. Potterton was called to the pastorate. He began his work September 1, 1892, and resigned October 1, 1893. A permanent parish organization was made January 5, 1893, with John E.

Cousens as president. Rev. Stephen H. Roblin took charge of the church at Mr. Potterton's resignation. September, 1894, Rev. Herbert E. Cushman became pastor, as successor to Mr. Roblin, and continued until January 1, 1896. In June, 1895, the chapel at the corner of Washington and Cypress streets was purchased from the Methodist society. Rev. Charles W. Biddle, D. D., became pastor September 1, 1896, and was installed October 25th.

The parish is fully organized for work on helpful lines, and is active in several departments of Christian effort.

PRESBYTERIAN.

The Presbyterian church held services in Brookline as early as January, 1894. Rev. C. S. Dewing became pastor in charge, and continued the services first in Harvard hall and later in Goddard hall. In September, 1894, Rev. William Elder Archibald, Ph.D., became pastor, and because of his successful ministry, and through his efforts, land was purchased in 1896 for a church on Prospect street. The work of construction was begun during the autumn of that year, and the corner stone was laid on Christmas day. The building was finished in the spring of 1897.

CONGREGATIONAL–UNITARIAN.
Christ's Church.

Christ's church, Colchester street, Longwood, was erected by Hon. David Sears in 1860, and dedicated June 30, 1862. It is a copy of a church in Colchester, England, which Mr. Sears then considered the ancestral home of the Sears family. Mr. Sears' object was to provide a church where all might worship " in the unity of the Spirit and in the bond of peace." He prepared a liturgy to be used by the preacher. Among the clergymen who have been connected with the church are: Rev. James M. Hubbard, in 1862; Rev. C. C. Tiffany, in 1863; Rev. S. B. Cruft, in 1864 and a part of 1865; and Rev.

Henry A. Miles, Mr. Cruft's successor, whose sermon in memory of Mr. Sears, January 22, 1871, has been printed. Rev. Caleb Davis Bradlee, a well known clergyman, took charge in April, 1893, after the church had been without a regular minister for about fifteen years. There is now a large congregation. The pastor resigned in April, 1897, after a most successful ministry. His farewell sermon was delivered April 25th, and on the last day of the same week (May 1, 1897,) he died.

POLICE DEPARTMENT.

In the autumn of 1857, a special police and night watch was appointed, to be under the direction of Mr. Augustus Allen. The hook and ladder house was used for temporary lodgers. In the years immediately following, a watch was on duty Saturday nights and Sundays. In 1870 about eight men were employed and the arrests numbered nearly 200 a year. At the annual meeting a regular day and night force was ordered. As early as 1860, Mr. John P. Sanborn had been elected truant officer, and in 1864 a constable. Until the force was enlarged, he remained the only regular officer, but with power to call upon the other constables. In 1870 he was made chief and in 1874 submitted his first written report.

Alonzo Bowman was appointed chief of police to succeed Mr. Sanborn in 1876, and so has already served over twenty years. The other officers of the force now (1897) are : First lieutenant, George F. Dearborn ; second lieutenant, B. Frank Bartlett ; inspector, Albert S. Paige ; first sergeant, Alonzo W. Corey ; second sergeant, Joseph J. O'Connell ; third sergeant, Edward J. Mealey, Jr. ; court officer, Albert S. Paige.

June 23, 1870, a vote was passed to appropriate $3,000, " to finish and furnish a police station in the new hose-house." In March, 1872, the selectmen were authorized to purchase a lot of land on which to erect a station. After an ineffectual attempt to have a new building, a committee reported April 14, 1873, in favor of altering the old Town Hall, which had been superseded by the new Town Hall in February of the same year, for a police station, a court room for the trial justice, and an evening school. The report was accepted and the department still occupies the building.

FIRE DEPARTMENT.

In 1788, Colonel Aspinwall and Lieutenant Crofts were chosen fire wards, the first mentioned in the records. The town relied upon Roxbury for help in emergencies, and in 1795 it was "Voted, to pay one-half of the expences of the repairs of the fire engine in futer." In 1829 a committee was appointed "to see what amount the town of Roxbury have allowed for the purchase of hose and buckets for the new engine Norfolk, and that this town meet them in any expense for the same, not exceeding fifty dollars." Brookline citizens subscribed $325 and Roxbury $150. The engine cost $400, leaving a balance to be used in building an engine house.

In 1839 a new engine, the "Brookline," built by Hunneman, was purchased for $900, and in March, 1842, the Norfolk was reported sold, after considerable trouble arising from the joint ownership of the engine with Roxbury. The "Brookline" was burned in 1843. These engines were manned by citizens who formed themselves into a company.

The present engine house on Washington street was built in 1871, on the site of the former building. In the same year the election of fire wards was discontinued, and a board of engineers was appointed by the selectmen.

Under the new arrangement Alfred Kenrick, Jr., became chief engineer, and J. Thomas Waterman was chosen clerk. The engine which took the place of the "Brookline" was still in use, after more than thirty years of service. There were at the time three organized companies.

The first steam fire engine was ordered in 1873, at a cost of $6,950, sufficient water supply having at last been provided.

Mr. Kenrick resigned in 1874; his successors have been J. Thomas Waterman, William B. Sears, Horace A. Allyn, Moses Jones, and George H. Johnson, who has served as chief since 1878. Francis F. Muldowney and E. Frank Proctor are now (1897) associated with Mr. Johnson on the board of engineers.

GEOLOGY.

By Daniel S. Sanford.

Brookline is situated at the center of the
Boston basin, a circular area, which from its
isolation and the uniformity of conditions which
have prevailed within it, may be regarded as a
geological unit. The history of the Boston basin,
as interpreted by Prof. W. O. Crosby, has been
the record of the slow accumulation of sediment
under alternating deep and shallow water conditions, interrupted many times by periods of
volcanic activity of varying intensity, and termin-
ated by a mountain-making epoch during which
the thick sedimentary beds were compressed into
great east and west ridges and lifted permanently
above sea level. Such a condensed statement
necessarily fails to give any adequate notion
of the long ages of slow subsidence, of the
frequent intervals of minor disturbance when

rock masses were fractured and displaced, and lava poured forth "a liquid flood" over the sea bottom, and, least of all, of the æons of time during which the uplifted rocks were subjected to the destructive action of mechanical and chemical erosion, until a further elevation of the continent ushered in the glacial period.

In all of these experiences Brookline shared, and the record of many of them is still easily decipherable. One does not need to cross the town's boundaries to find evidences of nearly every force known to geology. Heat and cold, fire and water and ice have done their work; volcanoes, earthquakes, glaciers, freshet and ocean have combined to make Boston's most beautiful suburb.

The conglomerate ledges of the town form the crest of the largest and most central of the parallel ridges mentioned above; the melaphyre beds in the northwest corner of the town are believed to be a surface flow of lava below and antedating the conglomerate; and the slate, which appears in a narrow synclinal trough near the Chestnut Hill reservoir, is perhaps the last remnant of an extensive deposit of slate which once overspread all the conglomerate, but was unable to withstand the erosive power of ice and water. In the section of the town east of Newton street and north of Clyde street there are several dikes, the largest, in Clyde park, being fully 90 feet wide.

The northern end of the town, or, to speak more exactly, Brookline village and the section east of Boylston street and Chestnut Hill avenue, is drift buried, no outcrop of rock appearing. The glacial waste, consisting in the valleys and on the plains of assorted sand and gravel, and of hills of unmodified boulder-clay, covers everything. No well-defined terminal moraine appears, but the numerous boulders, the kettle holes in Muddy river valley and the Longwood district, and the drumlins show the abundance of material which the retreating glacier dropped in this vicinity. If the drift could be removed we should doubtless find a continuation of the rock series observed in the upper part of the town, the trough of slate broadening and flattening as it passed under Longwood, the Back Bay and Boston, and the conglomerate dipping from either side beneath it.

An examination of the map accompanying this volume will reveal several glacial features. Corey, Aspinwall, Fisher, Singletree and several smaller hills, are of the same shape and have a common northwest southeast trend, their longer axes being parallel to one another and to the striæ on the rocks. The oldest highways suggest a like parallelism, since they follow the valleys between the hills. The precise way in which these drumlins were formed is one of the unsolved problems of geology. Babcock Hill, one of the few extensive gravel deposits in the town, was wholly unlike them in character and origin. Hall's pond, commonly considered bottomless, is a true kettle hole, made by the late melting of a mass of ice around which the retiring glacier piled drift material. Ward's pond and Jamaica pond are of similar origin.

The extent to which the early history of the town was determined and our life today is influenced by purely physical causes becomes apparent when we reflect that the swamps, the drainage, the streams, the position of the hills so much prized as places of residence, and the location of the first roads, were all determined by the way in which the glacier at its melting disposed of the great load of waste material with which it was freighted.

In the clay beds of the Longwood district the first settlers found the material for brick making, one of their earliest industries. On the plain, which stretches from Corey and Aspinwall hills to the Charles and Muddy rivers, and which is in fact a delta made of glacial waste, they found the richest pasture lands, and here, at a point where the first roads converged, sprang up the Punch Bowl village. The drift hills, though less fertile, when once subdued to cultivation, made farmland of enduring excellence.

Since the supply of gravel from Babcock Hill was exhausted, the town has used for the repair of its roads the conglomerate quarried from the Washington and Newton street ledges. Later recourse may be had to the Hammond street melaphyre beds, which will furnish a still better road metal.

The changes wrought by the growth of Boston have augmented rather than diminished the influence of the glacier upon our modern life, for the drumlins more than any one other physical feature of the town, have fixed its residential character.

THE HOME OF MRS. EDWARD S. PHILBRICK, WALNUT STREET.

A station on the "Underground Railway" in *Brookline*

BOTANY.

By Miss Emma G. Cummings.

Up to 1850 the larger part of Brookline was covered with a growth of native trees. Of these many fine specimens here and there remain; and there may still be found within its limits a majority of the trees native to Massachusetts, —a great variety, since in Massachusetts alone there are more species of trees than in any country of northern Europe.

Longwood derived its name from the strip of woodland formerly extending from Aspinwall avenue to the old milldam, now Commonwealth avenue. The largest tract of woodland, an area of about 500 acres, is bounded by Heath, Hammond, Newton and Clyde streets, where are to be seen white cedars and some fine large hemlocks and white pines. A smaller tract of about 50 acres extending from Boylston street to the line of the circuit railroad and Reservoir lane, has now growing upon it thirty different species of native trees, and many of them noble specimens of their kind : linden ; two maples, the red, and a giant sugar maple on the corner of Reservoir lane ; cherry, tupelo, ash, sassafras, elm, buttonwood ; four hickories, the shagbark or shelbark, mockernut, pignut and bitternut ; four birches, the black, yellow, white and canoe ; hornbeam, and hop hornbeam, not only plentiful in this region, but elsewhere in Brookline ; five different oaks, the white, swamp white, red, black and scarlet ; chestnuts, so large and old that they are falling to decay ; beech, white pine, pitch pine, hemlock, and red cedar. Some of these are represented by only a few trees. There are, besides, many of the smaller trees and shrubs, including shad, witch-hazel, cornel, alder, barberry, black alder (ilex), sumac, elder, viburnum, Benjamin bush, and willow. This is a region truly worthy to be preserved for the

education of the public. On the Longwood
playground are four tupelo trees, nearly all that
are left of a species once numerous in the low-
lands of Brookline.

Foreign trees have been planted along our
streets and avenues, such as Norway maple,
sycamore maple, European linden, English elm,
horsechestnut, and Norway spruce. But in
recent years, many native trees have been
planted, notably scarlet oak and elm on the
Beacon street boulevard; red, white, and pin
oak, sugar maple and white ash in the parkway,
besides in the latter place hundreds of shrubs of
the barberry, now thoroughly naturalized, cornel
or dogwood, and viburnum, showy at all seasons,
but especially the viburnum opulus, or high
bush cranberry, with its clusters of scarlet
berries in the autumn.

Have the wild flowers disappeared with the
encroachment of civilization? perhaps some one
will ask. Not altogether. Besides the commonest

wayside and wild flowers the seeker will still find growing hepatica, rue-anemone, marsh marigold, goldthread, columbine, corydalis, fringed polygala, cardinal flower, beech-drops, lady's slipper, Solomon's seal, dog's-tooth violet, trillium, and a great variety of goldenrods and asters.

THE BIRDS OF BROOKLINE.

By Reginald Heber Howe, Jr.

As one looks back at the Brookline of years ago when Muddy river meandered sluggishly between its less attractive banks, and Babcock's woods and many other places that have now been "improved" were wild and natural, when the cedar swamp lay, hardly known and unfrequented, under the shadow of Denny's hill, from the ornithological standpoint we regret deeply that that day has ceased to be. With the advance of civilization many birds have been deprived of their former homes. One can remember the day when "peep," marsh wren and rail were common along the creek, when red-winged blackbirds bred by hundreds in Babcock's swamp, and only a year ago a noted and extensive night heronry was to be found within the town limits.

We cannot complain at the irresistible strides of town improvement, nevertheless those who love the wild and natural portions of this favored place cannot help mourning the loss of some spot, the only home of a certain bird within our borders, when improvement meant not only the routing of that bird from that particular spot, but from the town altogether. The following list, incomplete as it must be, shows, however, what a wealth of bird life we still have and undoubtedly will have for many years to come.

Thanks are due Mr. Frederick H. Kennard of Brookline, Mr. Arthur L. Reagh of West Roxbury, Mr. Henry V. Greenough of Longwood, Mr. George C. Shattuck of Boston, and Mr. Francis H. Allen of West Roxbury, for kind assistance in the compiling of this list.

NOTE.— For explanation of reference marks see end of list.

1.   Podilymbus podiceps—Pied-billed Grebe.   Mr. William A. Eldredge shot a single bird on Muddy creek, in Longwood, about 1883.   6
2.   Anas obscura—Black Duck. Rare fall and spring migrant, Longwood-avenue marsh.   133

3. Anas discors — Blue-winged Teal. Mr. Allen noted a bird of this species on Weld pond, October 26, 1884. 140

4. Branta canadensis —Canada Goose. Migrant.‖ 172

5. Botaurus lentiginosus — American Bittern. Migrant.† 190

6. Ardetta exilis — Least Bittern. Formerly a summer resident.† 191

7. Ardea herodias — Great Blue Heron. Uncommon migrant.‖ 194

8. Ardea virescens — Green Heron. Summer resident. Known to breed just outside town limits.† 201

9. Nycticorax nycticorax nævius — Night Heron. Abundant summer resident and migrant, rare winter resident.‖ 202

10. Rallus virginianus — Virginia Rail. Formerly summer resident.† 212

11. Porzana carolina — Sora. Formerly common summer resident.‖ 214

12. Fulica americana — American Coot. Mr. Geo. R. Wales shot a single bird on Muddy creek, in Longwood, about 1883. 221

13. Philohela minor — American Woodcock. Migrant. [Rare summer resident.†] 228

14. Gallinago delicata — Wilson's Snipe. Uncommon fall migrant. ‖ 230

15. Tringa maculata — Pectoral Sandpiper. Uncommon fall migrant.‡ 239

16. Tringa minutilla –Least Sandpiper. Three birds taken at Weld pond, May 8, 1890.§‖‡ 242

17. Totanus flavipes — Yellow-legs. One bird, August, 1888, Weld pond. § 255

18. Totanus solitarius — Solitary Sandpiper. Common migrant.‖ 256

19. Actitis macularia — Spotted Sandpiper. Migrant. [§ Breeding near Weld pond, 1888.]§‡†   263
20. Colinus virginianus — Bob White. Permanent resident. ‖   289
21. Bonasa umbellus — Ruffed Grouse. Common permanent resident.‖   300
    Ectopistes migratorius — Passenger Pigeon. Formerly reported rare migrant.†   315
22. Circus hudsonius — Marsh Hawk. Summer resident.†‖   331
23. Accipiter velox — Sharp-shinned Hawk. [†Fairly common summer resident.] Common migrant.‖   332
24. Accipiter cooperii — Cooper's Hawk. Summer resident and migrant.†   333
25. Buteo lineatus — Red-shouldered Hawk. Common summer resident and migrant.‖ 339
26. Buteo latissimus — Broad-winged Hawk. Migrant.†   343
    Archibuteo lagopus sancti-johannis — American Rough-legged Hawk. A single bird was seen only a few hundred yards over the border line in West Roxbury — the bird undoubtedly entered Brookline.§   347a
27. Haliœetus leucocephalus — Bald Eagle. Accidental visitant.†   352
28. Falco columbarius–Pigeon Hawk. Migrant.‖
                357
29. Falco sparverius — Sparrow Hawk.‖   Rare summer resident. [§ Rare migrant.] 360
30. Pandion haliaëtus carolinensis — Osprey. Uncommon migrant.   364
31. Asio wilsonianus — American Long-eared Owl. Rare, permanent resident.†*   366
32. Syrnium nebulosum — Barred Owl. Rare, permanent resident.‖   368

48. Myiarchus crinitus—Crested Flycatcher. Summer resident and common migrant. ‖ 452
49. Sayornis phœbe — Phœbe.   Summer resident and common migrant.‖   456
50. Contopus virens — Wood Pewee.   Common summer resident. ‖   461
51. Empidonax minimus — Least   Flycatcher. Common summer resident. ‖   467
52. Cyanocitta cristata — Blue Jay.   Abundant, permanent resident.‖   477
53. Corvus americanus — American Crow.   Abundant, permanent resident. ‖   488
54. Dolichonyx oryzivorus — Bobolink.   Common summer resident.‖   494
55. Molothrus ater — Cow bird.   Common summer resident. ‖   495
56. Agelaius phœniceus — Red-winged Blackbird. Common summer resident. ‖   498
57. Sturnella magna — Meadow Lark.   Summer resident.   Breeding just outside town limits.   501
58. Icterus galbula — Baltimore Oriole. Abundant summer resident. ‖   507
59. Scolecophagus carolinus — Rusty Blackbird. Abundant spring and uncommon fall migrant.‖   509
60. Quiscalus quiscula æneus — Bronzed Grackle. Common summer resident. ‖   511*b*
61. Pinicola enucleator — Pine Grosbeak.   Common irregular winter visitant. ‖   515
62. Carpodacus purpureus — Purple Finch.   Resident, common migrant, winter visitant. ‖   517
63. Loxia curvirostra minor — American Crossbill. Common migrant.‖   521
64. Loxia leucoptera — White-winged Crossbill. Rare winter visitant.†   522

81. Guiraca cærulea — Blue Grosbeak.   One
    record " of a male taken in Brookline May
    29, 1880, by Mr. Gordon Plummer."   597
82. Passerina cyanea — Indigo Bunting. Common
    summer resident.‖   598
83. Passerina ciris — Painted Bunting. One record
    of a bird taken June 5, 1896. There is a
    chance, however, of this being an escaped
    cage bird.‡‖   601
84. Passer domesticus — English Sparrow.   An
    abundant resident.

    Carduelis carduelis — English Goldfinch.   I
    noted a single bird of this species in com-
    pany with a few American Goldfinches in
    May, 1892, in Longwood. There is a chance
    of this bird being an escaped caged bird,
    but it is probable that it was one of the
    Goldfinches or their offspring that were
    imported to this country not long ago.
85. Piranga   erythromelas — Scarlet   Tanager.
    Common summer resident. ‖   608
86. Progne subis — Purple Martin.   Occasional. §
                                         611
87. Petrochelidon lunifrons — Cliff Swallow.   [§
    Occasional.] [‖Formerly a summer resident.]
                                         612
88. Chelidon erythrogastra — Barn Swallow. For-
    merly common summer resident, now rare
    summer resident. ‖   613
89. Tachycineta bicolor — Tree Swallow.   Com-
    mon migrant and summer resident.‖ 614
90. Clivicola riparia — Bank   Swallow.   Occa-
    sional.§   616
91. Ampelis cedrorum — Cedar Wax-wing. Com-
    mon permanent resident, less common in
    midwinter. ‖   619

92. Lanius borealis — Northern Shrike. Common winter resident.‖ 621
93. Vireo olivaceus — Red-eyed Vireo. Abundant summer resident.‖ 624
94. Vireo gilvus — Warbling Vireo. Common summer resident.‖ 627
95. Vireo flavifrons — Yellow-throated Vireo. Common summer resident. ‖ 628
96. Vireo solitarius — Solitary Vireo. Common migrant and uncommon summer resident. 629
97. Vireo noveboracensis — White-eyed Vireo. Uncommon summer resident. 631
98. Mniotilta varia — Black and White Warbler. Common migrant. [† § Summer resident.]‖ 636
99. Helminthophila chrysoptera — Golden-winged Warbler. Common migrant. [Summer resident.§] 642
100. Helminthophila rubricapilla—Nashville Warbler. Common migrant. [Summer resident.§] ‖ 645
101. Compsothlypis americana usneæ — Parula Warbler. Abundant migrant.‖ 648
102. Dendroica æstiva — Yellow Warbler. Abundant summer resident. ‖ 652
103. Dendroica cærulescens — Black-throated Blue Warbler. Common migrant. ‖ 654
104. Dendroica coronata — Myrtle Warbler. Abundant migrant. [Rare winter resident.§] ‖ 655
105. Dendroica maculosa — Magnolia Warbler. Common migrant.‖ 657
106. Dendroica pensylvanica — Chestnut-sided Warbler. Common summer resident and abundant migrant.‖ 659

124. Troglodytes aëdon — House Wren. Local
summer resident.† 721
125. Troglodytes hiemalis — Winter Wren. Rare
migrant. One winter record. ‖ 722
126. Cistothorus palustris — Long-billed Marsh
Wren.‡ [Formerly common summer resident. Old Brookline marsh, now Leverett
pond.†] 725
127. Certhia familiaris americana — Brown Creep-
er. Common winter resident.‖ 726
128. Sitta carolinensis — White-breasted Nuthatch.
Common winter resident and rare summer
resident. ‖ 727
129. Sitta canadensis — Red-breasted Nuthatch.
Common migrant. ‖ 728
130. Parus atricapillus — Chickadee. Abundant
permanent resident. ‖ 735
131. Regulus satrapa — Golden-crowned Kinglet.
Common winter resident. ‖ 748
132. Regulus calendula — Ruby-crowned Kinglet.
Common migrant. ‖ 749
133. Polioptila cærulea — Blue-gray Gnatcatcher.
One bird taken September 8, 1887.§ 751
134. Turdus mustelinus — Wood Thrush. Common
summer resident. 755
135. Turdus fuscescens — Wilson's Thrush. Common summer resident. 756
136. Turdus ustulatus swainsonii — Olive-backed
Thrush. Common migrant.‖ 758a
137. Turdus aonalaschkæ pallasii — Hermit Thrush.
Common migrant. ‖ 759b
138. Merula migratoria — Robin. Abundant summer resident and uncommon winter resident.‖ 761
139. Sialia sialis — Blue-bird. Common summer
resident until severe winter of 1895. Now
regaining numbers.‖ 667

SUMMARY.

Species that have been noted within the town limits of Brookline by six observers since 1880, 139; species that breed within the town limits, 70; species that formerly bred within the town limits, 9; species noted in the Hall's pond region by three observers since about 1880, 100; species that breed within the Hall's pond region, 21; species that bred formerly within the Hall's pond region, 5.

Species that I have not noted, but which have been observed by Mr. Kennard, are indicated by a †; by Mr. Shattuck, by a *; by Mr. Greenough, by a ‡; by Mr. Reagh, by a §, and species that have no observer's mark following them I have noted, as have others in many instances. Species indicated by a ‖ have been noted in the Hall's pond (formerly Swallow pond) region (in Longwood), a wonderful *rus in urbe* for birds. Figures at the end of each paragraph indicate the American Ornithologists' Union check-list number.

THE TOWN HALL, WASHINGTON STREET.

NOTE.—Where no date is given the grant was made in the great allotment of January, 1636-7.

Alcock, Thomas, "his great allotment." 1636.
Aronsby, Edmund, great lot 3 heads. 1638.
Arratt, John, "great allotment." 1636.
Arratt, John, 10 acres.
Atkinson, Theodore, great lot 2 heads. 1640.

Bayter, George, 15 acres.
Beamsly, William, 16 acres.
Becke, Alexander, 8 acres.
Belchar, Edward, "great allotment." 1636.
Bendall, Edward, 35 acres.
Biggs, John, 8 acres.
Blackstone, William, 15 acres.
Blanton, William, carpenter, great lot 3 heads. 1639.
Bourne, Jarratt, 8 acres.
Bowen, Gryffen, great lot. 1639.
Browne, Edward, 8 acres.
Bulgar, Richard, 20 acres.
Burchall, Henry, 15 acres.
Bushnall, Francis, 24 acres.
Buttles, Leonard, bricklayer, great lot 4 heads. 1639.

Colborne, Mr. William, "his proportion of ground for a farm . . . . near unto and about his house." 1635.
Coulborne, Mr. William, 150 acres.
Coulborne, Mr. William, 10 acres marsh.
Coulbron, Mr. William, fresh meadow. 1639.
Cotton, Mr. John, "a sufficient allotment for a farm." 1635.
Cotton, Mr. John, "all that ground lying between the two brooks." 1636.

Cotton, Mr. John, 250 acres.
Courser, William, 10 acres.
Cramme, John, 16 acres.
Cranwell, John, 10 acres.
Curtys, George, great lot 2 heads.   1639.

Davisse, James, 10 acres.
Day, Mr. Wentworth, 100 acres.   1641.
Deming, William, 10 acres.
Dominqe, William, "great allotment."   1636.
Dyneley, William, 24 acres.

Eliot, Jacob, "swamp that joineth to his allotment."
   1648.
Elkyn, Henry, 8 acres.

Fairbancke, Richard, 24 acres.
Fitch, James and Richard, 16 acres.
Fletcher, Edward, great lot 3 heads.   1640.
Flint, Mr. Thomas, 24 acres marsh.   1636.

Griggs, George, 28 acres.
Grosse, Edward, lot 2 heads.   1640.
Grosse, Isaac, "great allotment."   1636.
Grosse, Isaack, 50 acres.

Harker, Anthony, 8 acres.
Heaton, Nathaniel, 20 acres.
Hibbins, William, 300 acres.   1640.
Hibbins, William, 10 acres.   1640.
Hollidge, Richard, great lot 3 heads.   1639.
Houlton, Robert, 16 acres.
Hudson, William, the younger, great lot 3 heads.   1638.
Hull, Robert, "great allotment."   1636.

Ines, Mathew, 8 acres.
Inge, Mawdit, great lot 3 heads.   1638.

Jackson, Edmund, 8 acres.
Johnson, James, 8 acres.

Kenricke, John, great lot 4 heads. 1639.

Leveritt, John, great lot 10 heads. 1639.
Leveritt, Thomas, [his] proportion. 1635.
Leveritt, Mr. Thomas, 100 acres.
Leveritt, Mr. Thomas, 15 acres marsh.
Love, John, "house plot and great lot." 1637.

Mason, Ralph, great lot 6 heads. 1637.
Mears, Robert, 20 acres.
Messenger, Henry, great lot 2 heads. 1639.
Mylam, John, 14 acres.

Offley, David, great lot 15 heads. 1639.
Oliver, James, 40 acres. 1640.
Oliver, Peter, 60 acres. 1640.
Oliver, Thomas, 100 acres.
Oliver, Mr. Thomas, 15 acres marsh.
Ollyver, Mr. Thomas, [his] proportion. 1635.
Olyvar, Mr. Thomas, fresh meadow. 1639.
Ormesby, Anne, 8 acres.

Painter, Thomas, joiner, great lot 4 heads. 1639.
Pell, William, 25 acres.
Pemmerton, John, 8 acres.
Perry, Isaac, house plot and great lot 2 heads. 1637.
Pormont, Philemon, 30 acres.
Purton, Elizabeth, 8 acres.

Reade, Esdras, a tailor, great lot 4 heads. 1638.
Reade, Robert, 8 acres.
Reynolds, Robert, 25 acres.
Route, Raphe, 12 acres.

Salter, William, 8 acres.
Saunders, Silvester, great lot 2 heads. 1637.

Savage, Thomas, 7 acres marsh.   1636.
Scottoe, Joshua, great lot 3 heads.   1639.
Scottoe, Thomas, "great lot 3 heads."   1637.
Scottoe, Thomas, great lot 5 heads.   1639.
Scottua, Thomas, small quantity.   1641.
Scottua, Thomasyn, 16 acres.
Sherman, Richard, great lot 7 heads.   1639.
Smyth, John, tailor, great lot 3 heads.   1639.
Snow, Thomas, 10 acres.
Snowe, Thomas, "great allotment."   1636.

Talmadge, William, "great allotment."   1636.
Talmadge, William, 15 acres.
Tappin, Richard, 24 acres.
Tinge, Mr. William, 500 acres.   1638.
Ting, Mr. William, 100 acres more.   1639.
Townsend, William, 8 acres.
Turner, Robert, 10 acres.
Turner, our brother, land.   1641.
Tytus, Robert, 20 acres.

Underhill, Captain, "great allotment of 80 acres."
    1636.
Underhill, Captain John, 4 score acres.

Walker, Robert, 14 acres.
Walker, Robert, 5 acres marsh.
Ward, Benjamin, 12 acres.
Wardall, Thomas, 20 acres.
Wheeler, Thomas, "great allotment."   1636.
Wheeler, Thomas, great lot 3 heads.   1638.
Wilson, Jacob, great lot 3 heads.   1638.
Wilson, William, 12 acres.
Winchester, Alexander, 20 acres.
Wing, Robert, great lot 4 heads.   1639.
Woodward, Nathaniel, the elder, 28 acres.
Woodward, Nathaniel, great lot 3 heads.   1639.

BROOKLINE CITIZENS IN 1679.

THE NAMES OF THE MALE PERSONS, LIVING AT
MUDDY RIVER (WITHIN THE TOWNSHIP OF BOS-
TON) WHO HAVE TAKEN THE OATH OF ALLEGIANCE.
[21ST APRIL, 1679.]

Edwd Devotion
John Devotion
Robt Grandy
John Parker Senr
John Parker Jun'r
John Winchestr Junr
Tho : Woodward Senr
Thom : Woodward Junr
Peter Aspinwall
Samll Aspinwall
James Pemberton
Joseph Pemberton
Michael Raseford
Tho : Gardinr Senr
Andrew Gardinr
Tho : Gardinr Junr
Joshua Gardinr
Caleb Gardinr
Ri : Woolfar
Christo Pigott
John Jennison
John Ackors
Edw : Chamberlyn
Jacob Chamberlyn
Dorman Morean
Isaac Heath Junr

Isaac Heath Senior
Jno Winchestr Senr
Ebenezr Hudson
Rosamond Drue
Clement Corbin
Iabesh Buckmaster
Jno Kelton
Jno Hubbard
Edwd Kubey
Joshua Kubey
Sam : Clarke
John Clarke
George Bersto
Jno White Senr
Benjn White
Jno White Junr
Joseph White
Jno Clarke
Uriah Clarke
Tho : Kelton
Tho : Boyleston
Mathew Preist
Tho : Kelton
Tho : Boyleston
Henry Segar
William Willis

Sam : Duncam	John Griggs
Joseph Davis	Edwd Cooke
Robt Harris	Tho Steadman
Tim^o Harris	Jno Sanall
Dan^{ll} Harris	Jno Stebbins
John Harris	Simon Gates

—[*From the manuscript "Record of the Suffolk County Court, 1671-80," now in the Boston Athenæum.*

FOUNDERS OF THE CHURCH, 1717,

As given by Dr. Pierce.

i. James Allen, Pastor elect,
ii. Thomas Gardner, Deacon,
iii. John Winchester,
iv. Joseph White,
v. Josiah Winchester,
vi. Samuel Sewall,
vii. William Story,
viii. Joseph Goddard,
ix. Thomas Stedman,
x. Joshua Stedman,
xi. John Winchester, son of iii.,
xii. Caleb Gardner, son of ii.,
xiii. Benjamin White, Deacon, son of iv.,
xiv. Samuel White, son of iv.,
xv. Amos Gates,
xvi. Ebenezer Kenrick,
xvii. Addington Gardner.

SISTERS.

xviii. Mary Gardner, wife of ii.,
xix. Joanna Winchester, wife of iii.,
xx. Hannah White, wife of iv.,
xxi. Mary Winchester, wife of v.,
xxii. Mary Boylston,
xxiii. Sarah Stedman,
xxiv. Desire Ackers,
xxv. Hannah Stedman,
xxvi. Rebecca Sewall, wife of vi.,
xxvii. Abigail Story,
xxviii. Mary Stedman,

xxix.   Sarah Winchester,
xxx.   Abiel Gardner,
xxxi.   Ann White, wife of xiv.,
xxxii.   Hannah Kenrick,
xxxiii.   Tryphena Woodward,
xxxiv.   Eunice Clark,
xxxv.   Mary Gardner,
xxxvi.   Susanna Gardner,
xxxvii.   Elisabeth Boylston,
xxxviii.   Elisabeth Taylor,
xxxix.   Frances Winchester.

PEWS DISPOSED OF APRIL 29, 1718.

i.   Samuel Sewall,
ii.   John Winchester, sen.,
iii.   Capt. Samuel Aspinwall,
iv.   Lieut. Thomas Gardner,
v.   John Seaver,
vi.   John Druce,
vii.   Joseph Gardner,
viii.   Josiah Winchester, sen.,
ix.   Thomas Stedman,
x.   William Sharp,
xi.   Ensign Benjamin White,
xii.   Benjamin White, jun.,
xiii.   Peter Boylston,
xiv.   Ministerial pew.

SOLDIERS IN THE CIVIL WAR.

A List of Brookline Men who were in the Army and Navy During the War of the Rebellion.

This list is intended to include the name of every man engaged on the Northern side who lived in the town from 1861 to 1865, or who could fairly be called "a Brookline boy" by birth or education. It is perhaps too much to hope that the list is entirely free from errors or omissions, since the original records give in each case the town enlisted from, rather than the residence.

ARMY.

Daniel D. Adams,
George Adams,
Edward F. Allen,
George E. Archer,
D. W. Atkinson,
George A. Bailey,
Pascal Barrel, Jr.,
Herbert S. Barlow,
Benjamin F. Baxter,
J. Nelson Bogman,
Robert Bowes,
William Bowes,
Alonzo Bowman,
George C. Burrill,
Edward C. Cabot,
Louis Cabot,
William L. Candler,
Charles D. Cates,
Michael Campbell,
Michael Canty,
Edward A. Chamberlin,
George B. Chamberlin,
J. H. Chamberlin,
Charles L. Chandler,

Burnham C. Clark,
John W. Clark,
Charles G. Colbath,
William B. Cowan,
Casper Crowninshield,
Bartholomew Cusick,
John B. Cusick,
Thomas J. Cusick,
James A. Dale,
P. Stearns Davis,
Samuel Dean,
G. F. Dearborn,
Fred Dexter,
Thomas Dillon,
Thomas Divine,
Charles Dwight,
Howard Dwight,
Wilder Dwight,
William Dwight, Jr.,
Charles A. Dwyer,
Horace N. Fisher.
John Herbert Fisher,
Frank Fitz,
Joseph W. Funk,
George W. Funk,
Patrick Gallagher,
J. Frank Getchell,
Louis G. Getchell,
Luther H. Gilman,
Warren H. Gilson,
William Goddard,
Charles E. Griswold,
William Gregory,
Willard Y. Gross,
Charles O. Hallett,
Llewellyn Ham,
William F. Hall,

John C. Hardy,
Nathaniel P. Harris,
Frank E. Howe,
Elisha A. Jacobs,
William H. Jameson,
Arthur Kemp,
John D. Kelly,
Malcolm G. Kittredge,
Alonzo B. Langley,
John Lawton,
R. C. Lincoln,
William E. Long,
Theodore Lyman,
John Lynch,
Michael Lynch,
Thomas Maloney,
Charles E. Maynard,
Charles B. McCausland,
John McEttrick,
Michael McGrath,
Charles McIntosh,
Frank H. McIntosh,
Frederick H. Mellen,
Jacob Miller,
Michael P. Mulrey,
Mark B. Mulvy,
Robert Murray,
William Nichols,
William W. O'Connell,
Henry Orcutt,
Mears Orcutt,
Charles L. Perry,
Edward S. Perry,
Julius A. Phelps,
Albert A. Pope,
George Pope,
Thomas Quinlan,

Hiram P. Ring,
Edward B. Richardson,
George P. Richardson,
James M. Richardson,
Spencer W. Richardson,
William C. Richardson,
William E. Richardson,
James F. Robinson,
George R. Rogers,
Charles E. Rollins,
George M. Rollins,
Edmund Russell,
Charles S. Sargent,
Aug. N. Sampson,
Daniel Sawyer,
Frank H. Scudder,
Henry B. Scudder,
William B. Sears,
Edward N. Selfridge,
Mark Wentworth Sheafe,
William (?) Sherriff,
Carleton A. Shurtleff,
Daniel W. Simpson,
James W. Sinclair,
George A. Slack,
Charles C. Soule,
George T. Stearns,
James P. Stearns,
Lyman P. Stephens,
George Stoddard,
George H. Stone,
H. V. D. Stone,

J. Kent Stone,
John Sweeney,
Clarence H. Thayer,
John Gorham Thayer,
Theodore Thayer,
Enoch Thomas,
Matthew Towle,
Charles Townsend,
Thaddeus J. Townsend,
Wm. Henry Trowbridge,
Joseph Turner,
Fergus B. Turner,
Osavius Verney,
E. Clifford Walker,
W. H. Warren,
Augustus Waterman,
J. H. Wellman,
W. L. Wellman,
Thomas Whalen,
William H. White,
Horace C. Whitfield,
B. F. Whitehouse,
C. H. Whitney,
J. H. Whitney,
Edward A. Wild,
Burt Green Wilder,
Alfred Winsor, Jr.,
Gershom C. Winsor,
James C. Withington,
John C. Withington,
Horace P. Williams,
John S. Woods.

NAVY.

John S. G. Aspinwall,
Charles L. Bixby,

—— Danforth,
Terrance Gallagher,

Joseph F. Green,
Winslow L. Hallett,
Frederic Hutchers,
Samuel G. Lamson,
D. F. Lincoln,
Patrick Linney,
Stephen Longfellow,
Patrick Mitchell,

John O'Dea,
Charles B. Pine,
Thomas O. Selfridge,
Thomas O. Selfridge, Jr.,
George G. Stoddard,
George Treadwell,
Henry W. Wells.

COMMISSIONERS OF PLANTATIONS.

Edward S. Philbrick,   Richard Soule, Jr.

NAMES OF MEN NOW IN BROOKLINE WHO SERVED FROM OTHER PLACES IN THE CIVIL WAR.

ARMY.

John H. Allen,
George L. Andrews,
Francis H. Bacon,
Erastus Blakeslee,
Watts H. Bowker,
John Carleton,
James W. Cartwright,
James Cass,
Amasa Clark,
Thomas W. Clements,
John Coffey,
William C. Cotter,
Ira B. Cushing,
Willard E. Daggett,
Henry C. Dimond,
Charles H. Drew,
Samuel W. Duncan,
Dana Estes,

William Finney,
Arthur Finnegan,
Charles G. Fowler,
Henry T. Hall,
Joseph W. Hall,
Charles D. Hammer,
Charles E. Hapgood,
David I. Harmon,
George E. Henry,
C. E. Hicks,
Eben W. Hilton,
Charles A. Hopkins,
Charles W. Kellogg,
Henry K. Langdon,
Augustus S. Lovett,
Henry S. Macomber,
Bernard Malone,
John Knox Marshall,

Albert Mason,
Alfred McKenna,
George W. Moore,
James S. Newell,
Castelly O. Norcross,
Phillip A. Nordell,
Henry K. Paine,
Isaac Paine,
Prince A. Phinney,
Charles A. Pons,
William Prée,
Andrew Robeson,
George R. Rogers,

L. Frederick Rice,
Alfred G. Sanborn,
William B. Sears,
Charles J. Seymour,
William P. Shreve,
William M. Snow,
Archibald Starkweather,
Edward Steese,
Charles Storrow,
William Stowe,
Thomas H. Talbot,
John A. Vining,
William B. Webber.

NAVY.

George E. Belknap,
John Cook,
Samuel D. Edwards,
Jeremiah Hayes,

Edward Holloran,
Cornelius Shannon,
Francis H. Swan,
William W. Swan.

POST OFFICE.

A post office in Brookline was established in 1829.

First.   Oliver Whyte, appointed in 1829.

Second. Stephen S. C. Jones, appointed in 1845.

Third.   James M. Seamans, appointed Jan. 1, 1851.

Fourth. Clark S. Bixby, appointed in 1852.

Fifth.   Alexander H. Clapp, appointed June 30,1855.

Sixth.   John McCormack, appointed Dec. 12, 1858.

Seventh. Cyrus W. Ruggles, appointed Sept. 30, 1865.

The office became a branch of the Boston office in 1883.

Isley M. Fogerty was appointed superintendent November 1, 1887.

The account books kept by Mr. Whyte are now in the Brookline Public Library.

PUBLIC LIBRARY TRUSTEES.

With the Years of Appointment.

Homer, George F., 1858–74.
Hovey, Edward C., 1888–92.
Howe, James M., 1857–62.
Lamson, William, 1864–75.
Lawrence, Amos A., 1857–62.
Parsons, Thomas, 1857–86.
Philbrick, William D., 1863–65.
Poor, Henry V., 1876–78.
Shedd, J. Herbert, 1864.
Shurtleff, Augustine, 1869–
Soule, Charles C., 1888–
Stanwood, Edward, 1892–
Stearns, Marshal, 1857.
Storrs, Leonard K., 1889–
Talbot, Thomas H., 1879.
Towle, George M., 1873–87.
Turner, John N., 1857–63.
Wellman, William A., 1859–63.
Wells, John, 1875.
Whitney, Henry M., 1877–78.

INDEX.